THE
FINAL
LIFE OF
NATHANIEL
MOON

A Middle Falls Time Travel Story

SHAWN INMON

The Final Life of Nathaniel Moon
by Shawn Inmon
Copyright 2018 © Shawn Inmon
All rights reserved

Printed in the United States of America

For Richard Bach, Piers Anthony, Robert Heinlein,

Frank Herbert, and Ray Bradbury.

I have learned so much from you.

Chapter One

Victoria Schmidt was engaged to be married on her twelfth birthday.

She was married in a secret ceremony on her thirteenth.

The ceremony was secret because, even with parental permission, minors under the age of sixteen were not allowed to be married in Minnesota.

The marriage was not Victoria's idea. She was opposed in every way, and made her opinion known as strongly as she was able. It did not matter, because the marriage had been arranged by Elijah Shepard, in his role as the Spiritual Leader of the New Believers movement, an offshoot of a spinoff of a splinter that derived from a faith no one could track back to its initial roots.

Mr. Shepard, who had been born Herb Finkelbaum, had nineteen wives, and took two new teen brides each year—one on the Summer Solstice, and another on the Winter.

When Victoria's father told her she was betrothed, she had said, "I won't go."

"You will," William said, removing his belt.

Bruised and battered, she went.

Victoria was repulsed by the groom Shepard had chosen for her—Dick Dillon, a fifty-six year old insurance salesman almost twenty years older than her father. His previous wife, Linda, had passed away the year before. The Coroner's Report had listed Linda's death as "death by misadventure," but the scuttlebutt around the New Believers compound was that her fall from the cliff while hiking had not been completely accidental.

The one blessing of the union was that Dick Dillon was diabetic, and had been rendered sterile a number of years before. His only offspring would be his son, Derek, who was three years older than Victoria, and who had moved away as soon as he turned eighteen. Derek had never adjusted well to having a stepmother who was younger than he was. Victoria suspected that although he paid it lip service, Derek was no more a True Believer than she was, which put his belief at approximately zero.

By her fourteenth birthday, Victoria was a wife in all ways but in the eyes of the law, and was charged with running a household. Over time, she took an interest in Dick's business, if not in Dick himself, and showed a natural aptitude with math and double entry accounting. Before she was sixteen, she took over the bookkeeping duties for his insurance office.

Dick Dillon was an unpleasant man by any standard. He wasn't attractive, with bad teeth, hair too scant to be called "thinning," and he somehow managed to be both too thin, with angular, jutting legs and arms, and too fat, with a heavy paunch that swayed when he walked. He was also given to bursts of anger that resulted in violence. While Derek was still living at home, it had been kept in check, but when it was just he and Victoria, it had escalated quickly. She had nowhere to run, no one to turn to.

The True Believers held to the idea that the man was king of his castle, and responsible for his own business within the castle walls, no matter what that might entail. That meant that even her own parents turned a deaf ear to her pleas, although her mother had the good grace to at least look pained as she turned her back on her only daughter.

Over time, Victoria became adept at reading moods at a glance and adjusting her own life accordingly, which kept the outbursts and violence to a minimum.

Victoria spent every minute thinking of how to make her escape, but she had no money and no way to get any. The only transportation she had was the '61 Mercury Monterey in the garage that barely ran, which Dick left for her to run errands around town, knowing it would never hold up for a longer trip..

Her indentured servitude lasted for nearly ten years. In December of 1978, just after Victoria had turned twenty-two, Derek Dillon returned home for an extended holiday visit. He hadn't been home for many years, and he had grown into a strong young man whose good looks reflected his mother's side of the family. On his arrival, he was shocked to find the young, spirited girl he remembered, cowed and quiet, meekly waiting on his father and doing as she was told.

When the elder Dillon went to work, and Derek and Victoria were left alone, she stood taller and became more like the girl he remembered. Derek saw the impact that life with his father had on her, and his heart went out to her.

Over the month-long visit, Victoria found what she never had before—kind words, a smile, shared conversation, and, inevitably, infatuation of a sort.

Over lunch one day, Derek said, "Did you and Dad ever get legally married?"

"No. From the time The Leader married us, everyone here considered us married, and that was all that really mattered to him. My dad mentioned it to him once after I turned sixteen, and he promised he would arrange for it. But then Dad died not long after, and it was never mentioned again."

Derek nodded, swirling his iced tea around the bottom of his glass thoughtfully. "That's not necessarily a bad thing, is it?"

Victoria flushed and cleared the dishes away, but Derek's deep blue eyes wouldn't leave her memory.

Over the next few weeks, nature took its course, and the two of them could hardly wait for Dick to leave for work in the morning. One afternoon, as they lay naked on the bed in the guest room, Derek said, "I know this has happened fast enough to make our heads spin, but love strikes like lightning."

Victoria considered. *Is this love? No, of course not. But, a smile and a kind word is so much better than anything else I've seen. It's closer to love than anything else I've ever known.*

"I've taken a job in Louisiana. When I get there, I'll be staying on company property at first, but by summer, I'll be able to be on my own. I'd love it if you'd come down and be with me."

"I'm sure there are a thousand pretty girls in New Orleans."

"None like you. I love you, Victoria."

Love was pledged, a pact was made.

Victoria agreed that if Derek would come back in a few months, when his father was away at work, she would be packed and ready to run. They both agreed that they would never see Dick Dillon again. With an eye toward that, Derek gave him completely wrong information about where he was going to work.

Derek left her with a few hundred dollars, nearly all the money he had in the world, in case she needed to get away sooner and come to him.

Victoria counted down the days.

A month later, on Valentine's Day, Dick was gone on a short business trip when Victoria awoke to the phone ringing and horrible nausea. When she answered the phone, she heard a recorded voice say, "Are you paying too much for your mortgage? We can..." before she realized she was going to throw up and hung up.

Victoria rushed to the kitchen sink and threw up the previous night's dinner. She hung over the porcelain edge for several minutes, waiting for the waves of dizziness and nausea to pass. Just when she felt like she could stand, the phone rang again.

She weaved her way to the phone and answered, "Hello?" There was a waver in her voice.

"You okay? You don't sound so good."

"I woke up sick this morning. Probably just a bug. I'm sure I'll be better now that I threw up."

"All right. My flight got delayed, so I won't be home until later tonight. You'll need to have dinner ready an hour later or so."

"Yes, sir," Victoria said, then numbly hung up the phone.

By the time Dick arrived home that night, she had thrown up half a dozen more times and was lying miserably on the couch, too weak to move.

She looked so poorly, Dick was afraid she might be dying, and quickly drove her to the emergency room. As the doctor examined her, she threw up again in a waste basket in the corner. He gave her a Promethazine suppository to stop the vomiting, which took effect quickly and gave her some relief.

Victoria, despite being in her early twenties and essentially a married woman for a decade, was still an innocent in many ways. The doctor was not. While he had her there, he took some blood so he could run another test and asked Dick and Victoria to wait there in the exam room.

For the purposes of the hospital visit, the doctor had been told that Victoria was Dick's daughter. When the doctor returned half an hour later, Victoria was already feeling a little better, sitting up, ready to return home.

"Feeling better?" the doctor asked?

Victoria, looking down at the floor, nodded.

"Good. Well." The doctor shifted from one foot to another. "I never know if this is good news or not, but I've found the cause of your nausea. You're pregnant."

Victoria's eyes widened and the color drained from her face, but she did not lift her eyes.

"Are you sure, doctor? That should be impossible." Dillon's voice was strained.

"There's always a chance of a false positive, even with a blood serum test, but it's highly unlikely, especially given her other symptoms—tender breasts and abdomen, vomiting." The doctor cleared his throat. "Well, there it is. I've written a prescription for more of the suppositories if the vomiting should return after this one wears off." He tore a sheet off his prescription pad and handed it to Dick, then hurried out of the room.

Dillon roughly grabbed Victoria and pulled her off the table. "Get your ass in the car," he whispered, his breath foul and hot in her ear.

It was a quiet drive back to the house they had shared for ten years. The wheels of Victoria's mind spun, but could find no purchase. *Pregnant.* As surreptitiously as possible, she moved her hand to her stomach. *Pregnant!*

Back at home, Dillon opened the passenger door and dragged her up the steps and into the house. As soon as the door closed behind him, he threw her down on the floor.

"You are impure. A Jezebel. Whore!" His voice grew louder with each word. He aimed a vicious kick at her midsection, but Victoria rolled on her side and absorbed the kick in her back. She cried out in pain.

If I lay here. He will kill me this time. He will kick me until I'm dead.

With a wince, she scrambled onto all fours and crawled away from him. She reached the couch and pulled herself up on all fours.

He was on her, raining his fists down on her head and shoulders, knocking her to her knees again.

"Stop!" she cried, holding an arm up to ward off the worst of the blows. She stumbled backward and fell across the couch. She looked up into his face, distorted with anger, tiny flecks of spittle clinging to his lower lip.

"This is your grandchild."

The truth of her words, and the realization of what that meant, pushed him beyond anger to insane rage. He fell on her, straddled her, and wrapped his hands around her throat. His lips pulled back from his teeth as he used every bit of strength he had to choke her to death.

Victoria pushed back, gasping for breath, but she was already weak and could feel her remaining strength draining from her.

She thought of her baby, so incredibly tiny, but already growing inside her.

Please, God. I don't care about me, but save my baby. Please.

It was her final conscious thought as Dick Dillon choked her until she died.

VICTORIA WOKE UP TO a telephone ringing loudly.

What? Where am I?

Her hands went to her throat, but there were no bruises. She swung her feet out of bed and realized she was nauseous. *And that damned phone won't quit ringing.*

She ran to the phone, paying for the effort with an increased wave of sickness in every step. She grabbed the phone and said, "Yes?"

A recorded voice said, "Are you paying too much for your mortgage? We can save you thousands of dollars over the life of..." before she slammed the phone down.

At that moment, she remembered everything. The throwing up, the doctor's visit, Dick killing her. She looked wildly around, but was alone in the house.

What in the hell happened? The last thing I remember is him straddling me, choking me, and then ... and then, I died. I know it. But, here I am. How is that possible?

The phone rang again, and she picked it up and said, "What now?"

Dick Dillon's voice came from the other end of the line. "Whoa, now. We've talked about the proper way to answer the phone. I know it's not a business, but sometimes clients call me at home, too, and we've got to treat them professionally."

"Huh? What?"

"Are you okay? You don't sound well."

"I'm not well. I'm sick. In fact, I think I'm about to throw up. I'm going to go."

"Just wanted to let you know my flight got delayed, so you'll need to delay dinner ... "

Victoria dropped the phone back in its cradle with a clatter and ran to the kitchen sink, where she threw up dinner from the night before.

There should be nothing left to throw up. I threw it all up yesterday. What the hell is going on? And why is he calling, acting like everything is normal?

Victoria's hand dropped to her stomach. *I'm alive. I'm pregnant. I'm living the same day over again. I don't know how, and it doesn't matter. I'm going to get the hell out of here. Now.*

She retrieved the money hidden in her closet that Derek had left her, grabbed a suitcase, threw a few clothes in, and ran to the garage. She stopped at the doorway to the garage to throw up again, but didn't bother to stop to clean it up. She paused and looked back into the house.

Anything else I want to take? Her eyes swept the kitchen, the door to the bedroom, the living room.

Nope.

Dick thought she couldn't go anywhere in the Mercury, because he took what he thought was the only key when he left town, but Victoria had made a copy of it two years before. She tossed her suitcase in the backseat and slid behind the wheel. She turned the key, trying to remember the last time it had been started.

The motor was sluggish, but eventually it turned over. She took a deep breath, put the car in reverse, and backed out of the garage, leaving the garage door open.

She drove straight to Highway 73, turned an hour south to Floodwood. When she looked at the gas gauge for the first time it was pegged past empty. She coasted into a Shell station on fumes, filled the tank, and picked up a road atlas, blowing a necessary part of her small resources.

Her nausea returned in a sudden tidal wave and she barely had a chance to open the door before she vomited again. She stopped at a small drug store, bought a bottle of Pepto Bismol and chugged a quarter of the bottle with a grimace. *Nothing else for it. I've got to keep going.*

She sat behind the wheel, considering. *Got to be smart about this. Where to? Derek, I guess. It's what I was going to do anyway. Can he protect me from his father, though? Would he kill both of us? Will he believe me that he already killed me once and I woke up just fine? Let's not worry about that.*

She connected with Interstate 35 and drove straight through until the needle on the gas tank once again approached empty. By then, she was in Iowa. Victoria filled up again, realized how little money she actually had, and began to cry.

She cried until she was done. *That's it. No more. It's not just me. This little person inside of me is relying on me now.*

She drove until she was too drowsy to go on, then found a rest area and pulled over.

Should have brought a blanket. I've got to start planning things out better.

Victoria opened the suitcase, found the warmest clothes she had brought, and put them on over what she was wearing, then bundled up in her coat and sat back down behind the steering wheel. She had a hard time relaxing, with people parking and moving around her, but eventually she began to drift off to sleep.

Just as sleep approached, she felt the baby inside her.

No way. It's got to be imagination. It's way too early for that.

It wasn't a physical kick she felt, though. It was an *awareness*. A feeling that she wasn't alone any more.

Out loud, she said, "Baby? Is that you? I can feel you."

Chapter Two
Dimension AG54298-M25736
1979

H e came awake, but did not open his eyes, for they were not formed yet. His body went on about its work, turning soft cartilage into bones, and building all the organs he would eventually need to exist outside his mother's womb. He paid this process no mind, but focused inward.

His first thoughts were of the life he had just left. His death was still fresh in his memory. He had been an old man, skin stretched paperthin, eyes watery, strength gone, surrounded by a family who loved him enough to let him go.

Susan. Thank you for letting me go. I was tired of the pain. I suffered from the limited perspective of the living. I didn't know what was next, but I was ready to find out.

He stretched his consciousness out, looking for what had occurred between letting go of his old body and beginning to build this one. When he focused his memory, he saw his life force leave the old body and move into a dimension invisible to the living. His watched his soul wriggle and frolic like a polliwog let loose in a fast-moving stream.

And then, he came awake, here, in his slowly building body.

Good enough.

He spent an unmeasured time reviewing that life. From the distance of a new life, he felt detached from the successes, the failures of what had once been so important. He dwelled on a few of his memories—his daughter's tiny hand wrapped entirely around a single one of his fingers as they walked along the shore of a gently lapping lake; standing in the bow of his fishing boat, lost in a sunset; sitting in a café with his friends. He savored the connections with those he loved.

He saw the times he had fallen down and failed both himself and those who loved him. He took those memories into his heart and held them tight. He wanted to carry them into this new life, so he would not repeat them. *Every mistake teaches us something, but if we refuse to learn it, then it's all for nothing.*

Beyond his most recent life was a long stretch of previous lives. He could look at any of them in as much detail as he wished, but simply skimmed through them. They were of interest to him in the same way an adult might look back on the early lessons of childhood—only in passing. He did notice patterns, though. Similar failures, similar triumphs, and made note of them.

He stood on the precipice of something new, and he was ready.

Inside his head, he heard a voice.

"Baby? Is that you? I feel you."

Mother.

Hello, Mother. Can you hear me?

"Oh! I can! What? ... I didn't expect this. Is this normal?"

A tinkling laugh filled Mother's mind. *You are asking me questions? I am only moments old in this life.*

"I just ... I knew you were special. I've felt it. But, I thought every mother believed their baby was special. I didn't expect ... this."

He reviewed through all his lives, from womb to death. He did not find any where he communicated with his mother before being born.

"Are you still there? Is this all in my imagination? I think I might be losing my mind."

I'm here. I was searching my past lives. This is unprecedented, at least for me.

"You can see your past lives?"

Yes.

"Will you always be able to see them? I don't remember anything about any life I've lived before—only this one."

I will forget. I do not want to bring too much into this life with me, or I will limit what I can learn.

"That makes me sad. Can you bring those memories with you if you wish?"

Yes.

"This ... forgetting ... is voluntary?"

Yes.

"Do you know other things? The secrets of the universe?"

There are no secrets. I know. You know, or at least you have known. We forget, so we can experience this life fully.

"Nathaniel?"

Is that my name in this life? He felt the word—*Nathaniel*—settle into him, become part of who he would be. *It's a good name. Thank you.*

"Will you do something for me?"

No answer.

"You are already so much smarter than me, Nathaniel, not answering until you know what I want. So, here it is. Will you take part of what you know right now, and make a place inside you where you can keep it safe? Somewhere you could find it again, if you wanted? Is that even possible?"

It is.

"Will you do it for me? We are all alone, you and I, and I am scared. I want to protect you, but I don't know if I will be able to."

Silence stretched out while Nathaniel looked at all paths that lay ahead and behind him.

I will.

"I only want what's best for you."

Our perspectives, when it comes to that, are very different. I'm going to be quiet now. There is much to do.

Victoria smiled inwardly, knowing what a blessing this child would be.

Nathaniel went about the business at hand—both forgetting, and building a place within himself where he could access all that is never truly forgotten.

Chapter Three
1983

Vivian Hanrahan, once known as Victoria Schmidt, sat in her cramped office, ledger books open in front of her and Nathaniel on the floor beside her, coloring. A small fan in an open window did very little to move the stultifying air. It was a little past 10:00 AM in Tubal, Arkansas, and it was already 91 degrees outside—the kind of heat that wraps around you like a thick wool blanket and makes breathing seem like too much work.

"Doesn't ever seem to bother you, though, does it, little man?"

Nathaniel looked up from his coloring and said, "What, Mama?"

"This heat." She fanned the front of her blouse, but the air refused to stir.

No. I like it. It feels right.

Tubal, just north of the Louisiana state line, was an unusual landing spot for a young woman from Minnesota. It was the town she had been passing through on the way to New Orleans, when her old Mercury had given up the ghost right in front of the *Get Gas Here* sign in front of Murdock's gas station and pizzeria. As it turned out, Bill Murdock also owned the wrecking yard in Tubal, and offered one hundred dollars cash for her car, which was likely more than it was worth.

By the time the sun went down on her second day in Tubal, she was gainfully employed as a seamstress at the Creech Coat and Uniform manufacturing plant just outside the city limits. She'd been pregnant, but still walked the two miles back and forth to work each day, until she had saved enough money to buy another old beater, just before Nathaniel was born.

Once she had a little bit of money saved, and a car again, she realized she could leave Tubal and finish her journey to Derek and Louisiana. A year had passed, though, and whatever infatuation she had once felt for him had dissipated.

Not long after that, Cyrus Creech himself had offered her the chance to get off the sewing floor and be his executive assistant and bookkeeper. Vivian accepted, as the floor was too damned hot five months out of the year and too damn cold another five months—April and October were blissfully moderate. Also, Cyrus Creech was a genuine family man and attached none of the strings to the promotion that many bosses did.

She almost never brought Nathaniel with her to work, but on this day, her sitter, Andi, had called her, sick with a summer flu. It had been too late to find anyone else. So, here they were, Vivian and her numbers and appointment books, Nathaniel and his colors.

Nathaniel had been born in Tubal, which may have explained why he didn't mind the heat and humidity. He stuck his tongue out of the corner of his mouth as he concentrated on coloring the green grass in his picture, when a racket from the back of the building attracted the attention of both of them.

Vivian's office was upstairs, on a catwalk that overlooked both the manufacturing floor and the shipping docks. She said, "Don't move, Nathaniel," and took one step outside the door of her office and peered down to see what had caused the commotion. Everything looked normal on the manufacturing floor. There were dozens of heavy-duty sewing machines operated by women with hunched backs and nimble fingers, making corduroy coats by the gross. The chaos and confusion came from the loading dock. From her viewpoint twenty feet up, Vivian could see a forklift tipped on its side, wheels still spinning. Heavy boxes had been knocked into a massive, jumbled pile.

"Oh, God," Vivian said. She turned, plucked Nathaniel up off the floor and hurried down the metal steps as fast as she could. At the back of the loading dock, half a dozen men were spread around the forklift, trying to lift it up, to no avail. Harry Spitton, who everyone called "Pup," was pinned beneath it. He was unconscious, with a thin dribble of blood coming from his mouth and nose.

Vivian didn't bother to ask what had happened. She just took control of the situation. She shouted, "Bob! Can you use the other forklift to move this one?"

Bob Mullen ran to the second forklift, fired it up, and maneuvered around the jumble of boxes until he was next to the tipped forklift. Two other men jumped in and fixed a strap around the forks of Bob's forklift and the cab of the second. Bob raised the forks until the strap was tense, then backed up. He didn't have enough torque to set it upright, but he did manage to lift the heavy machine a few inches.

Three sets of hands grabbed Pup and pulled him out from under.

Vivian took one look at Pup's prone form, then spotted Hazel, a middle-aged woman she had known when she worked on the sewing floor. "Hazel! Here, watch Nathaniel for me. I've got to go call an ambulance."

Hazel reached her arms out for Nathaniel. Vivian ran back up the metal stairs. There was no phone on the manufacturing floor. Hazel let Nathaniel slip down to the ground, but kept a hold on his small hand.

Nathaniel tipped his head to the right, so he could look around the knees of the man in front of him.

Pup stirred a little and Bob Mullen kneeled down next to him and put a hand on his shoulder. "It's okay, Pup. Just relax. Ambulance is on its way, and we'll get you to the hospital. You're gonna be just fine."

Harry's injuries weren't immediately obvious. There were no bones sticking out, or pools of blood beneath him. The forklift had landed mainly on his torso, and he was struggling to draw a breath. He was deathly pale. His eyes fluttered open, and he gasped out, "Can't breathe."

The crowd surrounding him looked from one to another. The extent of their medical training was a single class on mouth to mouth resuscitation that everyone had joked their way through.

While those around him dithered, Harry opened his mouth wide, a fish on a riverbank gasping for oxygen. He tried to lift his head up, but his eyes closed again, and his head slammed back into the concrete floor, unconscious.

At the back of the crowd, someone shouted, "Do mouth to mouth!"

Bob, who was kneeling next to Harry, laid a hand gently on Harry's chest and said, "I think his chest is crushed. I don't want to make it any worse. I'm gonna wait for the ambulance."

"He'll be dead by the time the danged ambulance gets here," someone muttered. They had drawn the word *ambulance* out into many syllables.

As Vivian hurried down the stairs, Hazel didn't notice that Nathaniel had let go of her hand. He was tiny and slipped between the men and women crowded around. He walked straight up to Harry and laid his small hand lightly on his chest, just as Bob Mullen had done.

Bad. It's all bad inside him. Somewhere deep inside him, something unlocked, unbidden, and rose to his conscious mind. *I can fix him.* For a brief moment, with his hand still on Pup's chest, Nathaniel closed his eyes and pictured him healed.

Bob looked down and saw him then. "Hey, there, who's this? Who do you belong to?" Bob picked Nathaniel up with one arm and looked around. "Whose kid is this?"

Vivian hurried forward and plucked Nathaniel away from Bob. "He's mine. Sorry." She touched Nathaniel's face and looked into his calm eyes. "You okay, honey?"

Nathaniel nodded softly. *Why wouldn't I be?*

Everyone's attention had turned to Nathaniel, and Harry lay momentarily forgotten. Forgotten until he opened his eyes and sat up. The color had returned to his face and he was breathing normally. "Holy shit, what happened to me?" Harry asked with amazement. He reached a hand up to dab at the blood around his nose and mouth.

Around him, everyone took a half step back, looking at a ghost.

In the distance, the whine of an ambulance siren slowly grew nearer.

"The boxes shifted on the forklift while it was on the ramp, and the whole shootin' match fell over, right on top of you," Bob said. "We thought you was a goner for sure."

Harry patted himself up and down as if looking for a missing pack of smokes. He shook his head. "Nope. I feel fine. Never better."

The stares of the crowd, wide-eyed now, turned from Harry to Nathaniel. Vivian cupped her hand on the back of Nathaniel's head and buried his face against her shoulder. "Good," she said in Harry's direction. "Glad you're feeling better." She cocked her head in the direction of the siren. "Ambulance will be here any second, though, and I want you to get checked out."

Harry shrugged. "Sure. No problem, but I'm pretty sure I'm fine."

Vivian, still holding Nathaniel against her, retreated to her office upstairs. She sat Nathaniel on her desk. He stared at her with his innocent blue eyes. "Nathaniel, honey, did you do something to that man on the ground? Did you help him?"

Nathaniel stared at her thoughtfully for a few seconds without saying anything.

Is this bad? You look scared.

Finally, he nodded.

"Do you know what you did?"

Silence stretched for several seconds, then, "I fixed him."

"Do you know how you did that?"

He shook his head. *No way to explain it.* "Just did it."

Vivian took a step back and drew a deep breath. She had waited for a sign, but after four years, she had stopped thinking about it as much. After Nathaniel had spoken to her before he was born, she had thought he might pop out of the womb speaking a dozen languages and solving advanced equations. He had been a normal baby, though, albeit what any mother would call a "good baby." He didn't fuss unless he was hungry, was sleeping through the night when he was only three months old, and self-soothed without a pacifier.

As Doctor Gray had said at Nathaniel's six month checkup, "If every baby was this good, we'd suffer from overpopulation, because everybody would want one."

Until that dripping hot July day, though, he had never done anything extraordinary.

A soft tapping on the door to her office startled Vivian from her thoughts.

"Vivian?" It was Cyrus Creech. He was a short, neat man in his mid-forties, given to dressing in linen suits and wearing hats that covered his thinning blond hair. For a time, he had also worn a wispy mustache, but his wife had soon taken care of that grooming faux pas.

"Yes, Cyrus?"

"So," he drawled, "I just got in the office, there's an ambulance in the parking lot, and I'm hearing some awful strange things." He glanced at Nathaniel, who was once again sitting on the floor, coloring his picture. "What in the heck is going on?" *Heck* was the strongest curse word Cyrus ever used.

"Honestly, I'm not sure. There was an accident on the loading dock. A forklift fell on Pup and we all thought he was hurt pretty bad, but once they lifted it off him, he seemed okay. The paramedics are checking him out to make sure."

Cyrus pierced her with a look, but just tapped his fingers against her door frame. "Okay, then. Find Bob Mullin, and send him up to see me, please."

Downstairs, the medics loaded Harry into the ambulance over his protests and took him off to the hospital five miles down the road in Dodge City.

Chapter Four

B y the next day, Andi had recovered from her summer flu, so she kept Nathaniel. Shortly after Vivian settled in for the day, Cyrus Creech appeared in her doorway.

"Viv? Can you come down to my office for a minute?"

"Of course. I'll grab my notepad."

"No need, just bring yourself."

Vivian stood up, smoothed the wrinkles from her skirt, and followed Cyrus down the narrow hallway to his office. The Creech Coat and Uniform building was, at best, utilitarian, and that extended to the President's office. The floor was covered in old linoleum, and the only furniture in the office were three filing cabinets, a large wooden desk with a swivel chair behind it and two wooden chairs in front. A picture of a waving United States flag hung on the wall. It was the only decoration in the room, aside from a hinged double picture frame with Mrs. Creech and his son, Byron on one side and a picture of Jesus on the other.

Bob Mullin was already seated in one of the wooden chairs.

"Please, Vivian, have a seat."

Cyrus moved around behind the desk, and said, "Now, we have a mystery on our hands here. You told me yesterday that a forklift fell on Harry, but after a few minutes, he was okay. That's borne out by the hospital, who said they couldn't find one thing wrong with him."

"Yes, sir," Vivian said.

"Now, Bob, here, has a slightly different take on things. He says that right after Harry was pulled out, he laid his hand on his chest to feel for a heartbeat, and that his chest felt like a bowl of oatmeal. Isn't that right, Bob?"

"As best I remember it, yes sir."

"It's difficult for me to reconcile how both of these things are so, even though it appears to be the case." He nodded at Bob. "Okay, Bob. Let's figure out what caused the accident in the first place and make sure it doesn't happen again."

Bob nodded, glad to be dismissed, and stood up to leave.

Vivian stood up, too, but Cyrus said, "Hold on a minute, Vivian." She sat back down.

Bob left and shut the door to the office behind him.

"Vivian, you've worked here for four years now. I know you, I know what kind of person you are. But this is a mystery, isn't it? The people who were there saw your little boy walk up to a man who was either dead or dying and lay his hand on him. A minute later, he was up walking around, right as rain."

"Cyrus, you know people believe a lot of silly things." She smiled. "Heck, people believe the Falcons are going to play good football this year."

The joke sailed high and wide.

"Have you ever noticed anything strange or unusual about your son?"

"Of course not," she shot back. Any trace of a smile instantly gone. "He's just a little boy."

Cyrus leaned back in his chair, steepled his fingers, and nodded thoughtfully.

"Fair enough, Vivian. That'll be all."

A WEEK WENT BY, THEN a month. A good month, in which Nathaniel produced no further miracles. He didn't turn his white milk into chocolate, nor did he walk across the municipal swimming pool when Vivian took him. She hoped that the "Miracle of Pup" would fade from everyone's mind.

That seemed to be the case until one evening in early August, when Cyrus Creech showed up on the porch of Vivian's small rental house. She was finishing dinner when the knock came on the door.

She opened it to find Cyrus dressed much more casually than normal, in a pair of khakis and a blue button-down shirt with the sleeves rolled halfway up, revealing thin, white arms.

Over Cyrus's shoulder, Vivian could see his late model Cadillac parked at the curb.

"Sorry to bother you at home, Vivian, but I just got back from Little Rock."

Vivian nodded. "Yes, sir, that's no problem."

Cyrus, his wife, and little boy had been making increasingly frequent trips to the Children's Hospital in Little Rock, but Vivian wasn't sure why.

Cyrus wrung his hands. "I know you're cooking dinner. It smells delicious. I hate to bother you, but could I come in for just a moment?"

Vivian stepped back and opened the door wide. "Of course, come in. Is Mrs. Creech with you?" Vivian asked, looking out toward the Cadillac.

"No, she's with Byron," Cyrus said, stepping across the threshold. He looked down at the floor, nervous about his errand. When he met Vivian's eyes, he looked as if he was in pain. "I really do hate to bother you, but it's important. Can we sit down?"

"Of course. Here, please take a seat on the sofa. I'll be right back, I just need to check on dinner. We're having meatloaf, which isn't Nathaniel's favorite, so he won't mind dinner being put back a bit." She glanced down at Nathaniel, who was looking at a picture book in the middle of the floor. "Nathaniel, put away your book, and say hello to Mr. Creech."

Vivian disappeared around the corner to the kitchen, and Nathaniel did as he was told, closing his favorite picture book, which had long-necked dinosaurs on the cover, and sat on the couch next to Cyrus. "Hello."

He is so sad. I feel the weight of it.

"Hello, Nathaniel." Cyrus reached out to shake Nathaniel's hand. "You like dinosaurs, eh?"

Nathaniel nodded and said, "Yes. Crocodiles are almost the same now as they were millions of years ago."

A small burst of surprised laughter came out of Cyrus. "Yes! That's right. You're a smart boy, aren't you?"

Nathaniel shrugged. "I saw it on a show." *Why do adults think kids are dumb? Just because we don't talk about something doesn't mean we don't know.*

Vivian reemerged from the kitchen, wiping her hands on a dish towel. She sat down in the chair next to the sofa, and said, "Okay, you have my undivided attention."

Cyrus nodded. "This is very difficult for both Alice and me. We haven't talked about it with anyone else, because that makes it even more real, but Byron has been a sick little boy for quite a while now. They're doing everything they can for him up at Children's Hospital, but today they kept him there." He paused and looked out the window, at the children running and playing in the street. "We're afraid he might not get to come home this time."

"Oh, Cyrus," Vivian said, scooting forward on the chair. "I didn't know. I'm so sorry. Is there something I can do at work to make this any easier for you? Any responsibilities I can take over?"

Cyrus looked at her bleakly for a long moment, as if he wasn't quite following. "Oh, oh no. We've got everything set up at the factory so that it's running like a finely-tuned machine. No, that's not it." He looked up at the old ceiling tiles, stained by years of previous smokers living there. He cleared his throat. "No, what I was wondering is ... Alice and I, that is ... we were wondering if you would mind riding up to Little Rock with us tomorrow, and bringing Nathaniel?"

Vivian sat back in the chair a bit. "What? Why? What in the world would be the purpose of that?"

Cyrus shook his head. "The thing is ... " His voice lacked strength, and tailed off. "The thing is, when you're faced with losing something, *someone* who means the world to you, even a tiny chance seems big. But we're even running out of tiny chances."

Vivian leaned forward. "I'm not following what you mean at all."

"You're going to make me come out and say it? All right. We're hoping that Nathaniel could do for Byron what he did for Pup."

Vivian sat all the way back, surprise etched on her face.

"Oh, Cyrus, you can't believe all that nonsense, can you?"

"It gets in your head, when you hear about a miracle and you need a miracle yourself. I would do anything if I could take this on myself, but I can't, and watching our boy slip away is the hardest thing I've ever done."

Vivian shook her head. "There wasn't a miracle. Nathaniel is just a little boy, and that's all I want him to be."

"I know it's likely that's all your little boy is, but it would mean everything to Alice and me if you would bring him to visit. Then we can put this out of our minds, and focus on just saying good-bye."

Vivian cocked her head. She looked at Nathaniel sitting quietly beside Cyrus on the couch. "I can't imagine what it would be like to be in your position." She drummed her fingers on the arm of the chair, made up her mind.

"All right. We'll come with you. But you've got to agree to just let Nathaniel visit Byron, nothing else. No hoodoo voodoo, no expectations. I sympathize with what you're going through, I really do. But, my first responsibility is to Nathaniel."

Cyrus flashed a relieved smile and, nodding, said, "Yes, I understand. Of course you don't want to expose him to that kind of pressure and expectations. If you'll just be willing to come with us to the hospital, that's all I would ask."

Vivian stood up and reached a hand toward Nathaniel, who hopped down off the couch and held it.

"Alice stayed up in Little Rock, of course, but I'm going to sleep at the house tonight. I'd like to leave for the hospital about 8:00 in the morning. Is that too early?"

Vivian nodded down at Nathaniel. "Eight? God, no. This little man is an early riser. We're up and at 'em by six every morning."

For a brief moment, it looked as though Cyrus was going to hug Vivian, but instead, he just smiled, nodded, and said, "I'll see you in the morning."

Chapter Five

It was an uncomfortable ride north to Little Rock. Vivian had packed puzzle books and comics to keep Nathaniel occupied, but conversation between the adults, which normally focused on production schedules, ordering raw materials, and keeping unions away from the workers, lagged. When the unstated aim of the trip was to find out whether a young boy could perform miracles unseen since Biblical times, chatting about lesser things seemed unworthy. And so they drove up Highway 167, past Hardee's, Kum and Go gas stations, and Waffle House restaurants, mostly in silence.

When they pulled into the parking lot at Children's Hospital, Vivian turned to Nathaniel in the back seat. "Unbuckle, honey, then we're going to visit with Mr. Creech's wife and son. He's very sick, so I'll need you to be a big boy."

Nathaniel unbuckled and stepped out of the cool of the Cadillac into the steamy late summer heat. He took Vivian's hand as they walked toward the hospital.

Once inside, Vivian's hand tightened as they followed Cyrus through the maze of corridors, turns, and elevators. His certain pace showed his familiarity with the facilities. Eventually, they stepped out of an elevator on the fourth floor and walked to room 426. At the door to the room, Cyrus held up a hand.

"I haven't talked to Alice since last night, so I'm going to go in and see how he is first, then I'll be right back out."

"Of course," Vivian said, as Cyrus stepped inside.

Nathaniel looked around the long hallway at the new environment. A green stripe was painted on the wall at his eye level. A nurse's station stood at the end of the hallway, an array of doors off to each side. Somewhere, the sound of a ventilator whooshed softly.

"I wish he'd have left us downstairs," Vivian said to no one in particular. "It's uncomfortable standing in a hallway like this."

Interesting though. Never seen any place like this. The vibrations are different here. I can feel so many worried, sad people.

Vivian brushed the hair out of Nathaniel's eyes. "We need to get you a haircut soon, don't we?"

Nathaniel smiled mischievously and shook his head. His bangs fell back in his eyes once again.

"I swear, when you smile like that, I don't know if you're an angel, or a devil."

Cyrus opened the door and stepped back into the hall. He shook his head and stared at the floor. "I don't know, Vivian. He did fine overnight, but he's taken a turn this morning. The doctors ... "

Vivian laid her hand on his arm. "I'm so sorry. We shouldn't be here." She came to a sudden decision. "Don't worry about us. I'll call Andi, and she'll come and pick us up. You've got enough to worry about without thinking about us, too."

Cyrus shook his head. "No. Alice still wants to try. I know we're grasping at straws here, but that's all we have left."

Vivian hesitated, but Creech kneeled down, looked Nathaniel in the eye. "You wouldn't mind just coming in and saying hello to my little boy, would you, Nathaniel?"

Nathaniel's wide blue eyes grew a tick larger.

Vivian sighed. "Really, this is a time for family." Cyrus stood back up. "But I understand. Okay, let's go in." She looked down at Nathaniel. "Just be quiet in there, okay, honey?"

Nathaniel nodded and took Vivian's hand.

Inside, the room was mostly dark. The shades were pulled, the overhead light was off. The only source of light in the room was the greenish glow from various monitors and a subdued recessed light over the bed.

Alice and Cyrus Creech stood together in a huddled puddle of misery and worry, looking down at their son. Byron Creech was three years older than Nathaniel. But laying in the hospital bed, he looked like a child heedlessly thrown into a dryer and allowed to shrink.

Alice Creech left Cyrus's side and reached out to Vivian. Her face was dry, but her eyes shone with tears recently cried. She had once been pretty, but now she was drawn and worry lines were deeply etched around her eyes. "Mrs. Hanrahan?"

Vivian nodded.

"Thank you so much for coming."

Nathaniel's head was turning on a swivel, taking in the strange beeps, antiseptic smells, and wires running everywhere. A small picture of Jesus was on the bedside table where Byron and his parents could readily see it.

"And this is Nathaniel, of course," Alice said. She reached down and lightly touched his head with a sad smile. "He's a healthy, beautiful boy."

Vivian took Alice's hand and held it between her own. "I'm so sorry, Mrs. Creech. I can't even imagine how difficult this is." She turned and took a step toward the bed and looked down at Byron. He had once been a blond, chubby little boy, but now was bald, with sunken cheeks. Vivian laid a hand on Byron's leg through the blanket. He didn't stir.

Nathaniel stared at the boy, but didn't approach him. Alice and Cyrus stood a few steps back, obviously praying for a miracle they couldn't imagine, but were doing their best to believe.

A long minute passed in silence, then Nathaniel moved to the head of the bed. He reached his mind out, looking for Byron.

For the first time since they had entered the room, Byron's eyes opened. He turned his head, so he could see Nathaniel, but his eyes were uninterested. Nathaniel cocked his head and held eye contact with Byron.

There you are. Oh, you are so sick. It's everywhere in you. It's killing you, and it is almost done.

He reached a hand out and laid it on Byron's shoulder.

Byron closed his eyes.

The numbers, flickering on the greenish monitors, were steady and unchanged. There was no opening of the skies, no hallelujah chorus. No anything.

Nathaniel removed his hand and looked up at his mother.

She reached down and picked Nathaniel up. She made her best attempt at a smile, failed miserably, and said, "I really do think it's best if we just find our own way home, Cyrus. Byron and Alice need you here. I'll call Andi to come pick us up, then we'll grab a bite in the cafeteria while we wait for her. Please don't worry about us."

Disappointment etched across Cyrus's face. He had known it was unlikely that Nathaniel could do anything for them, but now that even that slim possibility was gone, he was forced to face the reality of what came next. Cyrus reached in his back pocket, pulled out his wallet, and fished out a fifty dollar bill. "Thank you, Vivian. We appreciate that you came all this way. Please give this to whoever gives you a ride, for their time and gas."

Vivian considered, then took the money. "Not at all necessary, but I'll give it to her. Thank you."

She hugged Alice, who she had met for the first time less than five minutes earlier, as if she was a lifelong friend. She reached a hand out for Nathaniel, took a last glance at the quiet form in the bed, and led him out, so the Creeches could be alone.

Six hours later, somewhat worse for the wear, Vivian, Andi, and Nathaniel rolled back into Tubal. It had been a long day, and the longest time he had ever been seat-belted into a backseat. By the time they hit the Tubal city limits, Nathaniel was ready to do something. Anything.

They stopped at the Dairy Queen at the edge of town for chocolate-dipped ice cream cones, using the money Cyrus had given them. They walked across the street to the small park to eat them.

In the end, Vivian burned as much energy as Nathaniel, as she pushed him on the swing and the roundabout.

Finally, she retreated to the bench with Andi and watched Nathaniel chase after a grasshopper. "Doesn't seem to have affected him, did it?"

"No, he seems like his perfect little Nathaniel self," Andi answered.

"It's too bad this whole trip turned out to be a wild goose chase, and it would have been much better to have seen Byron stand up on the bed and do jumping jacks, but..." Vivian chewed the inside of her cheek. "But, I can't help but wonder. If that had happened, what would have been next? Would word spread about the miracle boy of Tubal? Would reporters and TV trucks have been parked outside our little house?" She shook her head. "I guess I'm glad that God, or fate, or whatever it is that controls this universe let life take its own path."

"Miracle boy, huh?" Andi squinted into the reddish glow of the setting sun. Nathaniel was running across the field, pretending to fly an imaginary kite. "I don't know. Looks like every other four-year-old I've ever met."

Chapter Six

Vivian held Nathaniel on her shoulder while she slipped the key into her front door lock and let herself inside. She dropped her keys on the kitchen table and carried Nathaniel into his bedroom. She laid him on his bed, slipped his tenny runners and clothes off, and found his Batman pajamas that he had worn the night before crumpled at the end of his bed.

"Won't win me Mother of the Year awards," she said, slipping the PJs over his head, "but I don't think anyone from the award committee is here in the bedroom at this moment."

"I like the Batman pajamas. I don't care if they smell kind of funny."

Vivian sniffed the PJ tops, then shrugged and helped Nathaniel under the covers.

"'Night, sweet boy."

"Night Mama. I love you whole tiger, whole world."

Vivian had no idea where that phrase had come from, but Nathaniel had been saying it as his highest compliment of devotion for months. "Whole tiger, whole world," she promised, brushing the hair out of his eyes for one final time on the day.

At the door to his room, Vivian paused and said a prayer of thanks for him.

She wandered out into the kitchen, found a half-empty bottle of wine she had opened the weekend before and poured herself a glass. She carried it out into the living room and considered turning the television on, but remembered there was never anything good on Friday nights. Instead, she sat on the couch, kicked her shoes off, and enjoyed the silence.

"I believe I could drift off right now, and not wake up until I hear the pitter patter of his little feet." Out of the corner of her eye, she noticed a blinking red light on her answering machine. She tried to ignore the light. "It'll still be there, blinking, in the morning." She took a long sip of wine and laid her head back. Vivian Hanrahan was not a woman who could let a blinking red light go unchecked, though, even with a little wine in her.

She dropped her feet off the coffee table, walked to the little side table that held her cordless phone and answering machine and pushed the playback button.

"You have one message," the automated voice said, followed by a beep. Then, a long hiss of static, before Cyrus Creech's voice came on. "Vivian, Cyrus." His voice was choked, but exhilarated. "It worked! By God, it worked!" Another long burst of static. "After you left, Byron slept for hours. His vitals didn't change. But—here's the miracle—when he woke up, he said he was hungry. Hungry! He hasn't been hungry in months. The doctor's going to come look at him again in the morning, but we can see. There's life in his eyes again. I don't know how, but that little boy of yours is a walking miracle! Proof of God's works in our world!"

Another pause, as the tape wound quietly on the microcassette in the answering machine. When Cyrus continued, he was quieter. "We're going to stay here in Little Rock until ... well, until things get sorted out. I have a feeling we'll be bringing Byron home with us when we come. Alice asked me to tell you 'Thank you, thank you, thank you' for bringing our boy back. I don't have to tell you what it means to us." A long beep signaled the end of the message.

Vivian pushed "Erase" on the recorder, picked up her glass of wine, and walked to Nathaniel's bedroom—a typical four-year-old's bedroom. There was a He-Man and the Masters of the Universe poster above his bed, edges curling. A toy box overflowed with Stretch Arm-strong and G.I. Joes, an Etch-a-Sketch and Hot Wheels cars. A book-shelf filled with well-loved picture books.

"Not the bedroom of a new messiah. Just a boy," Vivian said quietly, before crossing the room and pulling up the blankets Nathaniel had kicked off in his sleep. Standing once again in the doorway, looking at his small, sleeping form, she came to a decision.

"I'll do whatever it takes, Nathaniel, so you can have a normal life. Whatever it takes."

THE FOLLOWING WEEK was wonderfully normal for Victoria at Creech Coat and Uniform.

Mr. & Mrs. Creech and Byron stayed at the Children's Hospital for the week while the doctors ran batteries of tests, looking for answers they would never find. The end result was the same—Byron was once again a healthy child, with a happy smile for everyone who came to visit him. The Creeches didn't mind the delay, they were content to be a family and spend time together.

At the factory, life went on as it always did. Vivian kept her ear to the ground to see if there was any more talk of miracles and unex-plained cures, but aside from some employees remarking how wonder-ful it was that Byron was on the mend, all was quiet. Nathaniel's name never came up. Vivian stopped worrying about it for the moment and focused on smoothly running things until Mr. Creech returned.

When Cyrus did make it back, the middle of the next week, the first thing he did was make a quick trip around the manufacturing floor, theoretically checking materials, but really accepting well-wishes and congratulations. The second thing he did was summon Vivian to his of-fice.

She sat down across from him, notebook in hand. Before he spoke, Cyrus raised his hand to indicate silence, walked over and closed the door. When he sat back down, he smiled broadly and said, "The doctors can't explain it, but they've given Byron a clean bill of health. They may not understand it, but we do, don't we?" His entire attitude spoke of a happy conspiracy between them.

Vivian shifted in her chair, took a deep breath, and tried to decide how to proceed.

Before she could, Cyrus said, "This is big. Really big. Bigger than any of us." He stood and started to pace behind his desk. "Have you talked to your pastor about your boy, and what he can do?"

"We don't attend church."

Cyrus stopped in mid-step and turned toward her. "Really? Oh, I just assumed."

"I understand. Here we are, right in the buckle of the Bible Belt, so pretty much everyone goes to church, or feels guilty about it, but we don't. We had a bad experience."

"At church? A bad experience?" He shook his head. "Well, we don't have any of those here. Would you be willing to bring Nathaniel in to meet with Pastor Michaels at my church?"

"No."

Cyrus stopped, as if the answer had been a foregone conclusion. "No?"

"That's right. No. Look, Cyrus. It was against my better judgement that we went to Little Rock with you in the first place. I'm glad that something changed, and that Byron is going to be fine. I'm thrilled. But the most important thing to me is to protect Nathaniel. I can't do that by traipsing him out to strangers like a trained monkey. If you really are grateful to us, please just forget we had anything to do with it." She stood and closed her notepad. "Is there anything else you need from me?"

Cyrus appeared stunned at this sudden turn of events. Mouth slightly ajar, he shook his head.

"Thank you. I'll be in my office if you need me. I put the production reports there in your inbox."

Vivian let herself out, but as she walked down the hall toward her office, her hands were shaking.

Chapter Seven

T hat night, Vivian, Andi, and Nathaniel were settled in the living room. The adults were more or less watching an old black and white movie on TBS, and Nathaniel was staging a battle between his action figures and dozens of small green army men. The action figures were larger, but the army men had numbers on their side.

Andi had once been only a babysitter, but over the past few years, she had evolved into more of a member of the family. It wasn't unusual for her to stay for dinner, and then to still stick around and watch television and visit with Vivian. For her part, Vivian was glad to have another adult to talk to. Nathaniel was a bright young boy, but he was still only four, and more concerned with his toys than anything else.

Andi was draped across the chair, not really watching the movie, but not wanting to go home to her boyfriend, either. With a sigh, she slipped her legs off the arm of the chair. "Guess I might as well head for home. The longer I stay here, the worse it'll be when I get there." She paused. "Of course, if I wait long enough, he'll be drunk and passed out by the time I get there."

Before she had a chance to even slip her shoes on, there was a knock on the door. Vivian and Andi exchanged a glance. Andi raised her eyebrows: *Are you expecting company?* Vivian shook her head slightly and went to the window. On the small porch, she saw Cyrus Creech and a man she didn't know.

She turned to Andi. "It's just Cyrus and some other man. Wonder what in the world he wants now. Stay with me for a minute, will you?"

"Sure." Andi knelt down and began picking up scattered army men off the floor.

Vivian answered the door. "Hello, Cyrus, you're full of surprises, aren't you?"

Cyrus looked a little flustered, but said, "Hello, Vivian." He gestured toward the man standing slightly behind him. "This is Pastor Michaels. I apologize for dropping in unannounced like this. I hope you don't mind."

Pastor Michaels was tall and thin, with round glasses, and a hawk's beak nose.

Vivian cocked her head, but lacked the ability to be outright rude. She stepped back, opened the door, and said, "Please come in." As the men came inside, she shook hands with Pastor Michaels.

"Pleased to meet you, ma'am." He barely gave a glance to Vivian, though. His attention focused on Nathaniel, still scooping up army men. He kneeled down beside him and said, "Hello, young man. I'm Pastor Michaels, but I'd like it if you'd call me Jimmy."

Nathaniel looked up from his clean up duties and glanced at Vivian, who gave him a slight nod.

"Yes, sir." He met and held Michaels' gaze steadily.

"You have very good manners. It's nice to meet you, Nathaniel." He stood and dusted off the knees of his slacks. He looked at Vivian and said, "I really do apologize for barging in like this, ma'am, but I needed to see this miraculous young man with my own eyes." He glanced, sidelong at Cyrus, cleared his throat. "After what Cyrus told me, I couldn't help myself. I was so excited, I called the Bishop of our entire region, Bishop McCallister. He and I prayed about it, and we were moved by God to come and talk to you."

"Well," Vivian said, looking sharply at Cyrus, "No good deed goes unpunished."

Cyrus looked at his shoes.

"And what is it, exactly, that you want to talk to me about? Something about my *four-year-old* son, I would guess?"

"Well, yes. Bishop McCallister wanted to know if you would drive with me to meet him in Dallas tomorrow. He's really quite excited to meet Nathaniel."

"Goodness," Vivian said, slipping into her recently acquired southern accent, "Little Rock last week, Dallas this week. I'm becoming quite the world traveler."

Cyrus stepped forward and said, "Take as much time as you need away from work. You're pretty much indispensable there, I'll admit, but the Lord's work comes before all else. We'll figure everything out, don't you worry."

Nathaniel looked at his mother.

Vivian took a deep breath. Carefully, she said, "I can see how important this is to you. And I understand how special Nathaniel is. It's hard for me, because I want to keep him all to myself, but I really do understand." She nodded. "All right. If it's that important to you, I won't stand in the way."

Reverend Michaels and Cyrus Creech beamed at her. Andi looked aghast.

"What time do you want to pick us up?"

"It's quite a drive to Dallas, especially if we catch traffic. Would 9:00 a.m. be too early?"

Vivian looked beaten down, but resigned. "No, no, that's fine. Shall I pack us a lunch?"

"Oh, no," Michaels answered quickly. "The church will be proud to buy the two of you lunch. There's a Cracker Barrel just outside of Dallas. We can stop there, have some of their wonderful cornbread, and meet with Bishop McCallister by 3:00. We'll be back here before Nathaniel's bedtime."

"That's fine, then," Vivian said. "We'll be ready to go."

Pastor Michaels beamed at her again. It was obvious that this had gone much easier than he had anticipated.

"Well, we'll get out of your hair, then," Cyrus said.

"See you in the morning, Mrs. Hanrahan. And," he paused and graced Vivian with his most sincere smile, the one that loosened up the tightest wallet when the collection plate was being passed, "thank you." He finally noticed Andi sitting off to the side, jauntily tipped a finger against his forehead and said, "Ma'am."

A moment later they were out the door. Nathaniel moved to the window and stood on his tiptoes so he could see out. *They look happy. Thought Pastor Michaels was going to jump up and click his heels for a minute there.* He watched them get in Cyrus's Cadillac. The car started, the headlights turned on, and it pulled slowly away from the curb.

Vivian turned around to a glare from Andi. "I can't believe you're letting those Bible thumpers mess around with Nathaniel. What are you thinking?"

Vivian glanced at the clock. 8:30.

"I think I've got twelve hours to pack up anything we want to take with us and get out of here."

Chapter Eight

"So," Vivian said, turning to Andi with a quick smile, "whaddya say? Want to stay up all night and help me figure out how to fit my whole life into a Chevy Cavalier?"

"You're leaving? Like, *leaving* leaving?"

"I would never let them get their claws into Nathaniel. I was just trying to get them out of here as fast as I could."

"But, where will you go?"

"No idea. I was on my way somewhere when I broke down here. I would have moved on eventually, anyway. I've always known Tubal isn't my ultimate destination."

Andi looked thoughtful. She was twenty years old, a cute redhead who had been born in Tubal and had rarely been outside of Union County. The trip to Dallas had sounded like a major road trip. The idea of packing up everything Vivian owned and heading out for parts unknown, dazed her.

Vivian glanced around the living room, taking inventory of the couch, chair, and coffee table.

"I got all this stuff second-hand a few years ago, so it's no big loss. Whatever we don't take with us, you can have. I'll give notice to our landlord while we're on the road, and we've paid rent through the end of the month, so you'll have plenty of time to move whatever you want out. You can even move in here for a few weeks if you want some time away from Carl."

Vivian retrieved an empty box from the back porch and brought it to Nathaniel in his room. "We are going on an adventure tomorrow. We might not ever come back here, so I want you to pack whatever toys you love the most in this box, so we can take them with us. Understand?"

Nathaniel looked at the box, perhaps two feet square, then looked at all the toys scattered around his room. *Not much room. But there are always more toys.* He shrugged and said, "Okay, Mama," and went to work.

Vivian watched him pick up one army man or Hot Wheels car, consider it carefully, then place it either in the box, or back on the floor.

"Half an hour, Nathaniel, then it's off to bed with you, and whatever's in the box goes with us, whatever isn't, stays here."

Nathaniel didn't even hear her. In his mind, he was envisioning future battles that would be fought with the toys he brought, and he wanted to make sure he got the right ones. He picked up a kneeling army man with a bazooka on his shoulder and said, "We'll definitely need you," and dropped him in the box.

Vivian walked back into the living room carrying another empty box and a roll of box tape. Andi sat cross-legged on the couch, a thoughtful look on her face.

"What would you think if I said I wanted to come with you?"

That brought Vivian up short. "Huh? Your whole life's here in Tubal."

"My whole life?" Andi laughed and ticked items off on her left hand. "Carl. Not the best boyfriend in the world. He cares a lot more about SEC football, trucks, and going fishing than he does me, and I know he always will. Job. My job is working for you. When you go, so does the job. Parents? Mom's dead, and Dad moved to Texas for work three years ago. I'm lucky if I get a phone call from him on my birthday." She pushed down a third finger, then paused. "And you know what's really sad? I've lived here my whole life, and I can't even think of four things I'd be leaving behind."

"Well, if you're serious, you don't have a lot of time to think about it. Nathaniel loves you, and it would be so much easier if he didn't lose you right now, too. So, wow." Vivian shook her head. "Crazy how things happen so fast. A few hours ago, we were eating Hamburger Helper and trying to decide what to watch on TV."

Andi jumped off the couch. "So does that mean I can go with you guys? I'd miss you both way more than I'll miss anything else in this town."

"Yes, of course you can come with us, you're family. But, there's one other thing to think about. When we leave here, we leave everything behind. I don't know if they will, but Creech and Michaels might come looking for us, and I don't want to be found. That means no phone calls to old boyfriends, or anyone else. Is that too much for you?"

Andi was quiet for a moment, thinking. "I think Carl will miss me for about two days, then he'll probably hook up with Missy over at the diner. I've seen the way he looks at her when we go in for lunch. Yeah, I get it. If I had those guys looking for me, I wouldn't want to be found, either."

Vivian opened her arms, and Andi jumped to her, squealing. "Oh, this will be so much fun! I've gotta go pack."

"One suitcase," Vivian said. "We're not gonna have much room. The "Cadavalier" doesn't have much trunk space. It's a lot more reliable than that old Merc that got me this far, though."

Andi nodded. "Got it. Can I borrow it to run home? I don't want to walk through town carrying my suitcase."

Vivian tossed her the keys. "See you soon."

Andi bolted through the front door and ran down the sidewalk to the silver Cavalier parked on the street.

Vivian looked around the apartment. "What do I have room for?" In the end, she settled on photo albums, Nathaniel's baby book, his box of toys, and one suitcase for each of them.

She looked at the small pile in front of the door and smiled. "Pathetic, really," she said to herself. She peeked in at Nathaniel again, sleeping peacefully now. "And none of that stuff matters."

Chapter Nine

B y 5:00 a.m., the car was packed, and Vivian carried Nathaniel, wrapped in a blanket, to the backseat. She had left it empty, so he could stretch out and sleep on the trip. She made a pillow out of their coats and laid him down. Andi rode shotgun, and Vivian slid behind the wheel. She started the car and took one last look at the little house.

"First house where I was ever on my own. First house with Nathaniel."

Andi looked at her. "You okay?"

The mist of memory cleared from her eyes. "Yeah, let's face it. It was kind of a shithole." They laughed, she shifted the car into Drive and two minutes later, they were in the country. After a few miles, they hit a main highway and turned north. One tiny town after another appeared in the distance, then shrank into their rearview mirror.

"Still no idea where we're going?"

"Not really. Wherever the wind blows us, I guess. Creech might re-member that I was on my way to Louisiana when I broke down here, so that's out. He knows I come from Minnesota, and I wouldn't go back there anyway."

Vivian had never told Andi why she had left Minnesota and she still didn't.

"So, that leaves east or west. Any preference?" Vivian smiled and looked at Andi.

"In school, I saw this picture once, of an amazing lake. It's got the clearest water you can imagine, so you can see more than a hundred feet down. I've always wanted to see it."

"What was it called?"

"Crater Lake. I think it was in Oregon." She pronounced it as Or-uh-gone, with the accent on the last syllable.

"Sounds like the closest thing we've got to a plan. What do you think, bug? How does Oregon sound?

Nathaniel paused, as though he had actually heard of either Crater Lake, or Oregon. In his head, he saw lives spread out before him, branching from many different paths. He was quiet for a few seconds, then said, "Good."

Vivian nodded. "Then to the west and Crater Lake it is."

AT 8:45, PASTOR MICHAELS pulled up in front of Vivian's house. There was a brown paper bag beside him that had candy bars, Pop Tarts, a six pack of Coke, and an oversized handful of Pixie Stix. He had no idea what a four-year-old ate, or what that much sugar might do to a child stuck inside a car on a four-hour drive, as he had no children of his own. He rolled the top of the brown bag over several times and sat it on the floor. "We'll keep that as a surprise if our miraculous boy gets antsy."

He sprang out of the car and took the steps up to Vivian's front door two at a time. He knocked—*shave and a haircut, six bits*—and waited. He knocked again, and this time noticed the slightly hollow echo from inside. After thirty seconds, he stepped off the porch and peered in the window. It was dark inside, but he could see a spray of newspapers, discarded boxes, and a lonely stuffed dog sitting on the floor.

"Good gosh darn it," Michaels said under his breath. He ran back to his car and sped off. Three minutes later, he was in his office in the church—nothing is more than three minutes away in Tubal, Arkansas.

He picked the phone up, dialed a number by memory, and said, "Hello? Cyrus, please." A few moments later, he said, "She's gone."

Michaels heard heavy silence on the other end of the line. "What should we do?" Creech finally said.

"What we should always do. Let's pray." Michaels closed his eyes. "Almighty Father, thank You for the gift of this day, and for bringing us into the presence of another of Your miracles. We have felt moved by You to bring this boy into Your grace, so these miracles can be shown to the world. But, he's controlled by a woman who is a non-believer. We seek Your counsel, Lord, Your direction. Bring the light of Your understanding to us. Amen."

After a momentary silence on both ends of the line, in a subdued voice, Creech said, "Meet me tonight at my house. We'll see what we can do about this. That boy is a reflection of the glories of God. We can't see his gifts wasted.

BY MID-MORNING, VIVIAN, Andi, and Nathaniel had two hundred miles between them and Tubal. Nathaniel had munched through a peanut butter and honey sandwich and a banana, and was happily letting his hand ride the waves of air out the back window.

By lunchtime, they were in Fort Smith, Arkansas, and Vivian drove around until she found a branch of her bank. Fifteen minutes later, over the protests of the local manager, she had closed out her account and walked out with a wad of cash—the result of four years of cheap housing, only drinking cheap wine, and no other bad habits.

She slid behind the driver's seat, waved the cash at Andi, and said, "Okay, we're not rich, but this will get us wherever we need to go. I've been adding to my *Go To Hell* fund for four years, a little bit at a time, and today's the day we say, 'go to hell.'"

As they sped out of Fort Smith, Andi rolled her window down and yelled, "Goooo Toooo Hell, Arkansas!"

Chapter Ten

Pastor Michaels pulled up in front of the Creech residence a little after 7:30. The Creeches lived in the nicest house in the nicest neighborhood in Tubal. In truth, the neighborhood wasn't all that much, but the house was a beautiful, two story colonial.

Michaels knocked on the door. Mrs. Creech answered and showed him in to the den. Cyrus Creech sat behind a bigger, more ornate desk than anything he had at the factory. "Come in, Pastor, come in. Please, sit down."

Michaels sat in the chair opposite and looked around the room. There was a lot of dark wood grain and pictures of the Creeches doing fun things as a family—a shot of them with skis and wind-burned faces, another of them standing proudly beside a huge swordfish hanging from its tail – as well as the obligatory picture of Jesus hanging where Cyrus could see it from behind his desk.

"You have a lovely home, Cyrus."

"Thank you. So, what are we going to do? Just let this whole thing evaporate?"

"I've thought about it all afternoon, but I'm coming up empty. What else is there to do?"

"There's always something to be done, if you've got enough drive and aren't afraid to commit."

"Look, Cyrus, I'm not sure what you're thinking, but the church can't be part of anything that's not completely above board."

"Of course, of course. That goes without saying. I would keep you out of anything like that."

Michaels shook his head. "No, that's not what I mean. It's not a wink-wink, nod-nod kind of thing. I was as excited as you were about bringing that boy to church headquarters, but she's his mother. What she says goes." Michaels cleared his throat and looked out the window. "I'm sorry, Cyrus, but I've got to go. I've still got a sermon to work on for Sunday."

Cyrus looked at him, disappointment etched on his face, but said, "Of course. Thank you for stopping by. We'll just let it go."

Michaels nodded. "No need to see me out. See you Sunday."

Cyrus didn't answer, but sat motionless at his desk for long minutes, his head bowed in prayer. Quietly, he said, "What would You have me do, Lord? I am Your servant." He closed his eyes and waited for an answer.

Eventually, he opened his eyes, scooted closer to the desk and pulled his Rolodex close. He flipped through the cards, and settled on one that said, simply, "Security." He punched the number into the phone on his desk. As soon as the man answered, Cyrus said, "J.R.? This is Cyrus. I need you to come to my house, ASAP," then hung up. He leaned back in his chair and put his hands behind his head to wait.

An hour later, a late-model blue Buick pulled up in front of the Creech house. A man in his early forties emerged from the car and walked up the sidewalk. He was the kind of man that anyone would have a hard time giving a description of, ten minutes after they met him. There was absolutely nothing remarkable about him, although that was somewhat remarkable in itself.

Cyrus didn't wait for the man to come to the door, but opened the door and waited for him on the porch.

"Hello, J.R. Thanks for coming so quickly. I've got a challenge for you."

"That's why I get up in the morning. I love a challenge."

Cyrus handed him an envelope. "There's your retainer. If you need more, let me know. This is of utmost importance, and I don't want to let money be the reason it doesn't get done. Understood?"

"Yes. What's the job?"

"It's a woman and her son. The woman worked for me until today. I need her found. Absolutely no harm can come to them, but I need to know where they are." Creech handed a file folder over. "This is everything I've got on her. She left this morning, so she's got about a twelve hour head start on you."

J.R. opened the folder and looked at the black and white picture of Vivian Hanrahan. He riffled through the pages that were attached. "Looks pretty thorough. Not a pro. Shouldn't take me too long to find her."

FOR THE NEXT THREE days, Vivian, Andi, and Nathaniel wandered across America. Andi, who had never been more than a hundred miles from Tubal, was in heaven. She gawked at long, flat fields of waving grain, the hills and lakes of the Ozarks, and the endless string of truckers who honked and waved at her long, slim legs from high above. Nathaniel didn't care about anything, as long as they didn't run out of peanut butter or juice boxes.

They spent their fourth night on the road at a small roadside motel in Kimberly, Idaho, a tiny town a few miles from Twin Falls.

They were on the second floor of the motel. Nathaniel was already asleep when Vivian checked a small calendar she kept in her purse. She turned to Andi and said, "Wait a minute, is today your birthday?"

Andi flushed. "Yeah, I was hoping you weren't going to remember."

"Why?"

"'Cuz we're on the road like desperados running from the law, and I didn't think it was important."

Another thought occurred to Vivian. "Holy heck, it's not just your birthday. It's your *twenty-first* birthday. I don't care if we're being chased by a posse like Butch and Sundance, a girl only turns twenty-one once." She scooped her keys off the nightstand. "You stay here with Nathaniel, okay? I'll be right back."

Fifteen minutes later, Vivian returned, swinging a brown paper bag. "Come on outside, I found a couple of chairs and set 'em up."

Outside, on the small walkway that looked over Highway 30, there were two plastic lawn chairs with a small table and ashtray between them. Vivian set the ashtray on the ground, then reached into the bag like a magician pulling a rabbit out of a hat. She pulled out a four-pack of Bartles and Jaymes wine coolers and sat them on the table. Next out was a package of Hostess Cupcakes and a lighter. Lastly, she retrieved a small twig she had snapped off a tree on the edge of the parking lot. She stuck the twig in one of the cupcakes and attempted to light it like a birthday candle.

"The '76 station had a good variety of wine coolers, but their supply of birthday candles was surprisingly low."

"Surprisingly," Andi agreed.

No matter how long she held the flame to the twig, it was too green to burn.

"Okay, you'll have to use your imagination. Make a wish, and blow."

Andi looked thoughtful. "I don't think I need a wish. For years, I had just wanted to get out of Tubal, and now, here we are, in nowhere, Idaho. Wish granted."

Vivian twisted the cap off one of the wine coolers, and handed it to Andi.

"Peach, huh?"

Vivian looked down at the bottle in her hand and said, "Yeah. I might have overstated how good their selection of wine coolers was. It was this, or beer."

"Excellent choice, and we both know peach spritzers pairs nicely with cupcakes." She devoured half a cake in a single bite. "Mmmm. That's good. Thank you, Vivian."

Vivian uncapped a bottle for herself, tapped bottles with Andi, then leaned back in her chair and stretched her legs out so her feet rested on the metal railing. Andi did the same, and they spent a quiet minute looking up at the stars and the full moon, which cast subtle shadows all around them.

Without looking away from the sky, Vivian said, "This can just be a vacation for you, you know."

"What do you mean?"

"I don't know what's ahead for us. You don't know where we're going, because *I* don't know where we're going. So, if you want, we can drive on to Crater Lake, then I can find a bus depot somewhere, and I'll buy you a ticket back to Tubal. Absolutely no hard feelings."

"And I would never see you, or Nathaniel, again."

Vivian considered that. "Likely true, although this life has taught me to never use the word never." Her smile reflected the moonlight.

Andi was silent for a long time before she said, "Two things. I love you and Nathaniel, so I'm not leaving you. Second, this isn't my first drink."

"I would have guessed. I don't think many kids in small towns wait until they're twenty-one for their first drink. However, it is your first *legal* drink, and that's something."

A car rolled by on the highway below.

"Thank you. I appreciate you giving me the chance, but I really do want to stay with you guys."

"We love you, too." They sat in silence for a few minutes, listening to the sound of a far off car approaching. "Andi, I'm afraid. I don't know how to stop Nathaniel from doing what he does. I don't really even want to. It feels wrong to be blessed with an ability like this, and to hide it under a bushel basket. But I also don't want to have him treated like a freak, or to have to pick up and run every time he 'fixes' someone. We'll run out of places to run, eventually."

"He listens to you better than any kid I've ever seen. I think you just need to have a talk with him. Maybe explain that he needs to talk to you before he fixes someone. We can even tell him why. He's so smart. He'll get it."

"You're likely right." Vivian drained her peach cooler, considered for a moment, but eventually twisted the cap off the second one. "I'll be peeing peach for a week, but what the hell. Oh, one more thing to think about. Wherever we go, we're going to need new names. I don't want to make it too easy for anyone to find us. You should keep Andi, so Nathaniel won't be too confused, but we need a new last name for you."

"You too?"

Vivian nodded, looked up at the moon, hanging so low in the sky. "I've always loved the name Violet. I think that's my name from now on. Violet Moon."

"Violet Moon," Andi said, letting the words roll around on her tongue. She looked at Vivian, considering. "Yes, it fits you." She drained the last of her first wine cooler, uncapped the second and said, "There's something really weird I want to tell you. I don't think you'll believe it, but if we're going to be family, I don't think we should have any secrets."

Chapter Eleven

"Well, now you've *got* to tell me," Vivian-who-was-now-Violet said.

"And, I already wish I hadn't said anything." A rueful smile played on her lips. "I have this terrible fear that after I tell you this, you're going to stick me on that bus back to Tubal, kicking and screaming."

Violet reached across the table and touched Andi's hand. "Family, remember?"

"Right. Okay. I've told you that my mom died three years ago, right?"

Violet nodded.

"The night she died, I wandered out of the hospital in a daze. My dad was so broken up that he wouldn't leave her, even though she was dead. I felt completely adrift. Mom was everything to us. It wasn't just that she handled everything, although she did. She took care of the money, did the shopping, planned and cooked the meals. The only time my dad had ever been in the kitchen was to grab another beer. But it wasn't that. We could figure out how to handle all that stuff, of course. I was a big girl, eighteen at the time. It was so much more. I knew she wouldn't be there to help me get dressed on my wedding day, or hold her first grandbaby. It was the hole she left in our family. It was like she was the sun, and Dad and I revolved around her. With her gone, we had no direction."

"Of course," Violet said, although she had never experienced a mother like that herself.

"So that night, as I stumbled out the front doors of the hospital, I lit up a cigarette—"

"—I didn't know you used to smoke!"

"—Oh, it was so much worse than just smoking. So. There I was, totally stunned and helpless, crying my eyes out, but doing my best to hide it, when this old pickup truck pulled right in front of me. It was this boy from town named Joey. He was a scumbag, but he was kind of cute. You know the type?"

"Only from movies. I had a pretty restrictive upbringing. But yes, I know the cute, bad boy type. Go ahead."

"Joey was more than just a bad boy. He was the worst kind of boy. And especially the worst kind of boy for a broken-hearted girl to run into right after her mom has died. I tried to brush him off, but Joey didn't brush off easily. He was a complete asshole, but he did have his charming side, too, and it was on full display that night. Long story short, I ended up getting in the pickup with him and going for a ride. You know how one thing leads to another? You are looking at Exhibit 1-A for that concept."

Andi was quiet for a moment, lost in the memory. Violet stayed quiet, let her stay lost for a time.

"I told him what had happened, that Mom had just died, and he acted concerned. Then, he said he had something that would make me forget all about the pain for a little while. We're all responsible for our decisions, and I know it. So it was my own choice. If it hadn't been Joey Fitzsimmons right then, it would have likely been some other bad boy the next day or the one after. I was primed and ready to lose myself. Which I did. I knew what the right thing to do was, and I did exactly the opposite. I knew I needed to get out of that truck and go find my Daddy and grieve with him. And that was just too damn sad."

A silent tear slid down Andi's cheek.

"Joey had this little tin of Altoids that he kept in his glove box. He said that was where he kept his big guns, and I needed something big that night. I told him he was absolutely correct, and I took whatever he gave me and washed it down with a hit from his beer bottle. It was warm. The beer, I mean. Gross."

Violet, who had been tearing up herself, laughed a little. "The things you remember."

"Joey told me that by the time we got to the party he was going to, I wouldn't feel a thing, that it would all just fade away. Truer words were never spoken. I don't remember much of anything after that, for a few years. It was like one big blackout."

Violet cocked her head. She was doing the math, and things weren't adding up, but stayed silent, to let the story play out as it would.

"Everything I remember from those years is just like little flashes, and none of them were good. Let's just say that my standards for what acceptable behavior was, fell to an all-time low." She shook her head to clear the cobwebs of those flashes from her mind. "About two years after Mom died, I knew where I was headed, and I finally decided to do something about it. I went to Daddy and asked him for help. He didn't have a lot, but he paid for me to go to a rehab center over in Texarkana. It was good. Thirty days there, thirty days clean, because I made sure I loaded up on the drive there."

Finally, Violet couldn't hold her tongue any longer. "I don't understand, Andi. By this time, you would have been watching Nathaniel for me. None of this fits together."

Andi raised her hand. "Ladies and gentlemen of the jury, please wait until all facts are presented before coming to a verdict."

Chastened, Violet sat back in the lawn chair and waited.

"I came out of the rehab center and moved back in with Dad. I was fired up, and determined to do things right. I got a job at Dairy Queen, stayed away from all my old friends. Went to my outpatient sessions. I did it all. And you know what? Addiction is so powerful. A month after I got out of rehab, I went to my old dealer and loaded up again. But,

I made the mistake a lot of junkies make. I used the same amount I was using before I got clean. My body couldn't handle it."

She looked straight into Violet's eyes.

"I overdosed. I died. I was alone in my childhood bedroom, so there was no heroic rescue, no Narcan, no anything, except for oblivion."

Violet rubbed her arms vigorously. There was a sudden chill in the air. She didn't dare ask what happened next.

"And then," Andi continued, "I opened my eyes, and there I was, back on that bench in front of the hospital, smoking a cigarette. Joey Fitzsimmons pulled up in his old truck, just like before. It was like I had started over. *Because I had.*"

She peeked over at Violet to see how she was receiving this confession, but Violet seemed lost in memories of her own.

"At first, I figured that I had just killed myself the night before, and now this was my reward, that I was going to have to relive all the biggest screw-ups of my life, over and over. This time, no matter how persistent he was, I told Joey to go screw himself, then waited for whatever was next. But, what was next was nothing. I sat there a long time. Eventually, Dad left Mom and came out and found me. We went home together. The weirdest thing was, that all-consuming addiction—that terrible need I had felt—was just gone."

Andi drained the last of the peach cooler and set it down with a little more of a thump than she meant to and jumped a little.

"I was still sad that Mom was dead, of course, but to me, it had been three years since she had passed. I focused on trying to help my dad, but he was too distant to reach. About a year later, he took a job in Texas. I think he just wanted to get away from the memories. To make ends meet, I got that same job back at the Dairy Queen. They were impressed that I already knew how to run the ice cream machine."

Andi laughed again, and this time, it was a more authentic laugh—no bitterness.

"A few weeks after I started working at DQ, I took a break and walked across the street to the park to watch the kids play. That was when I met you and Nathaniel. You know the rest of the story."

Andi leaned her head back against the webbing of the lawn chair. "I have never told anyone any of this, because I knew they would think I was deluded, but it's the truth, and I wanted you to know it. So, you gonna send me on the next bus home?

"No," Violet said. She thought back to the night Dennis Dillon had strangled her, and how she had woken up the next morning as though it had never happened. She rarely thought of it anymore, because what was there to gain by thinking about it? "Of course not. You know what, Andi-girl? I believe you."

This sincere expression of belief made Andi break down and cry an ugly cry, but it swept so much out of her, that she was glad to have it gone. She wiped her tears away with the back of her sleeve, and said, "You wanna know something? After I met you and Nathaniel, I started to believe that maybe I was given a second chance just so I could help him. I still believe that."

Violet laid her hand on Andi's and said, "Me too."

Chapter Twelve

Nathaniel slept late the next day, which was a blessing to Violet and Andi, who had stayed up late into the night. By the time they got packed, breakfasted, and on the road, it was after 10:00.

All of which conspired to mean that they didn't make it to Crater Lake that day. Instead, they found a cute lodge-like motel at Klamath Falls, and stopped there. They spent the evening hiking along a fast-rushing stream that cut through the pines behind the lodge, inhaling the clean, cool air.

Nathaniel led them on the hike, saying over and over, "I like this place, Mama," as he bent to pick up a crawling bug or interesting rock.

Andi said, "You know, I like this place, too. Everything here feels so different—like something out of a movie." She waved her arm in an arc, taking in the entirety of the forest. "Living in Tubal, I couldn't even imagine something like this was even out here."

On the walk back to the room, Vivian picked Nathaniel up, kissed his cheek, and said, "I need to talk to you about something, honey, and it's really important. Get your good listening ears on, okay?"

Always, even when you think I'm not listening.

"Okay, Mama."

"Do you remember when you fixed the man that had been hurt at Mama's work?"

Nathaniel let his mind wander back. *That felt good. Right.* He nodded.

"And the little boy you fixed at the hospital?"

I wasn't sure I could do it with the first man, but when I fixed the boy, I knew. He was harder, but it felt right, too.

Another nod.

Violet paused, still looking for the right words. "I want you to talk to me before you fix someone like that. Understand?"

Why?

"It's not bad, Mama. They felt wrong, and I made them right."

"I know you did. It's not bad at all. Never think that. I don't think you could do something bad if you tried. It's just that other people can't do that. They can't fix people like you can."

Why not?

Nathaniel furrowed his brow. "They can't?"

"No, honey. I can't. Andi can't. You're the only person I know who can, because you are so special. So, it's not bad at all, but before you do it, I just want you to talk to me first."

"Okay, Mama." Nathaniel lifted his arms, slid down, and ran ahead of them on the trail, looking for more weeds and flowers he could pick to make a bouquet.

Violet looked at Andi and shrugged. "No idea what sinks into him, and what doesn't."

The next day, they were back on their early-rising schedule and pulled into Crater Lake National Park by 8:30 am. The visitor center wasn't open yet, so they drove on up a steep gravel drive until they found a place to pull over.

They hiked up a small rise and when they reached the top, the entirety of Crater Lake spread out before them. Violet and Andi were chatting about possibly changing their hairstyles when they saw the lake. The vast perfection of it mesmerized them and cut their words off in mid-sentence. Even the easily distracted Nathaniel stopped and stared. The three of them stood stock-still, staring with their jaws slightly unhinged for quite some time.

Violet turned to Nathaniel to see if he wanted to be picked up so he could see better, but saw that tears were running down his cheeks. Alarmed, she kneeled in front of him. "Honey? What's wrong?"

Nathaniel just shook his head, causing more tears to run. He pointed out at the pristine water in the caldera. "Look," was all he said. Violet swooped him up in her arms and held him tight. She whispered, "I love you, Nathaniel," into his ear.

They spent the next few hours circling the lake on the thirty mile loop road, stopping every few hundred yards to get a new perspective on the lake. They ate a picnic lunch of bananas and string cheese at a table warmed by the late-summer sun.

"I don't know how I've never heard of this place," Violet said. "Everyone should come here. Thank you for thinking of it, Andi."

"My one good idea for the trip. Everything else is on you now. Speaking of which ... "

"Do I know where we're going next? Not a clue. We'll drive until we see a nice little town somewhere, and that will be it. I don't want to live in a city. I want Nathaniel to grow up where it's safe for him to play outside, and where he can have friends to ride bikes with."

"And, where we don't have to worry about some religious zealot wanting to turn him into the poster boy for God."

"Yes, that too."

They packed the remains of their lunch away, stopped at the visitor's center and watched a film about how Crater Lake had been formed thousands of years earlier, although it happened very recently in geologic terms, then hit the road.

A few hours down the road, dark clouds rolled in and heavy raindrops spattered against their windshield. Violet turned the wipers on, and they drove west through the pouring rain. Each night, they had pulled off the road by dinner time, since they had been in no hurry to get anywhere in particular. On this night, though, they grabbed hamburgers at a roadside drive-in and continued on.

They drove alongside a lazy river that twisted through bucolic farm country, then up and across a mountain pass. Eventually, they connected with Interstate 5. Nathaniel gave up on the idea of a comfortable bed and laid down across the backseat, using one coat for a pillow and another for a blanket.

As the clock approached the witching hour, Violet saw an off ramp ahead.

"I think that's enough of a trek for one day. Not sure what this place is, but it's got one thing going for it—we're here."

They took the exit, curled around and saw lights twinkling in a valley below them. They dropped down toward the warmth of the lights. As they drew near, they saw a green and white sign: *Middle Falls, Oregon. Population, 41,261.*

"Middle Falls," Violet said, rolling the name around on her tongue, trying it on for size. "I didn't see the beginning falls, or the ending falls, but apparently we've found the middle falls." She glanced at Andi, still alert in the passenger seat. "How's he doing back there?"

Andi glanced into the back seat. "Out like a light."

"Let's drive around and see what Middle Falls has to offer."

They drove toward the brightest lights until they found downtown Middle Falls, such as it was, after midnight on a weekday. The normal businesses were present and accounted for—Rexall drugstore, liquor store, law office, accounting firm, veterinarian's office, movie theater, and bookstore. All were closed and dark at this time of night. There was no sign of movement anywhere.

"Quiet," Violet said, then added, "That's a good thing."

At the end of the block was a Safeway grocery store, also dark.

"I guess if you live here and run out of milk at night, you're just out until the next day."

They turned away from the business district and drove through several neighborhoods. Mostly single-level houses with small yards. Most of the driveways had five or ten-year-old cars or trucks sitting in them.

Violet drove toward the edge of town, past a bar called *The Do Si Do*, and spotted a motel with a *Vacancy* sign lit out front. Violet turned into the parking lot, turned off the engine and looked at Andi. "Kind of an anonymous looking little town, which ain't all bad for someone looking to stay anonymous."

"I like it. It's cute. And, it's a lot bigger than Tubal."

Violet nearly said, "Everyplace is bigger than Tubal," but instead, she smiled and said, "I think maybe we're home."

THE PHONE RANG ON THE desk in the home office of Cyrus Creech. He picked it up on the second ring. "Creech."

"Creech, J.R."

"I thought it was about time I'd hear from you."

"Yes, sir. Unfortunately, I don't have much. I bribed the girl who worked at the local branch of her bank to look up her account. She closed it up in Fort Smith, the same day she left Tubal. She had a balance of," the sound of papers rustling as J.R. looked for the number, "a balance of $3,822.48. After that, she disappeared. No sign of her. We put out a nationwide trace on her vehicle. No sign of it anywhere, yet. If she sells it, or so much as gets a traffic ticket, I'll know about it within twenty-four hours."

"What else?"

"Not much, unless you want me to randomly hire people to go to different parts of the country showing her picture. That's a needle in the haystack, and gets expensive very fast."

"Do this. Put one more man on the team, looking for her. It's important, and I'm willing to pay the freight."

"Yes, sir, will do. I'll call you next week."

Creech hung up the phone and looked across at his wife.

"Why go to all this trouble?" Alice said. "Especially after what she and her little boy did for us? They obviously want to be left alone. Why not let them live their life, and we'll live ours?"

"That would feel selfish. He saved our son, but we let them allow other children to die, when they could possibly be saved?"

"It's obvious that they don't want to live that life."

"*Heal the sick, raise the dead, cleanse lepers, cast out demons. You received without paying; give without pay.* Matthew, Chapter 10, Verse 8," Cyrus said.

"*Each one must give as he has decided in his heart, not reluctantly or under compulsion, for God loves a cheerful giver.* Second Corinthians, Chapter 9, Verse 7," Alice retorted with a grim smile. "Let's not have a biblical argument. You know I always win those."

Cyrus grinned ruefully. "You're right about that, my dear, but not about this. When I think of the gifts that child possesses, the idea that God gave him so much, and that he would squander it, it's impossible for me to allow." He reached out for Alice. "You have a good heart, and I know you only want the best. That's what I want, too. Even if a little persuasion is needed."

Chapter Thirteen
1989

Miss Haywood finished writing *The Oregon Trail* on the blackboard, then turned to the class.

Miss Haywood was in her forties, with brown hair that was showing the first signs of gray, which was pulled back into a severe bun. She never wore makeup, and had worn the same style cat's-eye glasses since college. She believed they would eventually come back into style.

"We'll finish our History studies for the year with the Oregon Trail. Who can tell me where the Oregon Trail began?"

Mary Billings raised her hand, but Miss Haywood patiently waited. Mary always raised her hand, and most times, Miss Haywood ended up calling on her. Still, she always hoped one of the other students would perhaps look the answer up and give her another choice to call on.

The fifth grade class of Middle Falls Elementary only had another month of classes, and the hearts and minds of many of the children were already directed outside, where the sunny weather made them all feel it could be summer now and they should be outside.

Nathaniel Moon sat halfway back in the classroom. He knew the answer to the question, as he had become interested in the Oregon Trail over the summer, and had read a number of books about it from the Middle Falls library. He tended not to raise his hand and answer the questions, though, unless he sensed that Miss Haywood was fed up with calling on Mary. He was reading ahead in their textbook, looking to see if there was anything in there that he hadn't read over the summer. One of the books he had read had told him that there were spots where the ruts from wagon wheels were still visible, and he hoped to see a picture of such a place.

Behind him, the largest boy in the class, Jon West, looked over his shoulder and watched him turning the pages of the textbook. Saying that Jon was the largest boy in the class was a vast understatement. Jon was the largest boy in the same way that Alaska is the largest state. Both are true, and both are true by a lot. He wasn't fat by any means, just large. His father was 6'4 and 240 pounds and his mother wasn't much smaller. Jon was already looking like he would eventually pass them by.

Miss Haywood was just about to give up on the waiting game and call on Mary, when the bell rang, dismissing the students for the day. The moribund students sprang to life as though electricity zapped their posteriors.

"Please read Chapter Eighteen in your History textbook, so we can discuss it tomorrow," Miss Haywood said, over the scraping of chairs and chatter of conversation. Few heard her, and fewer still paid her any mind.

The last two students to leave the classroom were Jon and Nathaniel. As Jon left, he glanced over his shoulder and saw that Nathaniel was speaking to Miss Haywood. Speaking, not really as a child speaks to a teacher, but almost as an adult who had wandered into an elementary school classroom. Jon shook his head, and lingered outside the classroom, watching him.

Jon had been watching Nathaniel all school year, trying to figure him out, and he hadn't come close to succeeding. Most kids, it was easy to figure out what their thing was—to be a jock, or a brain, or just trying to skate through school until real life kicked in after a few more years. Nathaniel defied all easy categorization. He was kind, and bright, but was not easy to push around or bully.

Nathaniel saw that he and Miss Haywood were alone in the classroom, but continued his conversation with her. He had noticed that she had grown increasingly sad over the course of the year, and now, near summer break, she had seemed to not care about anything at all. Nathaniel saw her glance up at the clock, so he excused himself to leave, but before he did, he reached out and laid his hand on hers, a gesture of childlike innocence. He returned to his desk, put his books away, then retrieved his accordion so he could take it for his lesson and left.

Miss Haywood sat at her desk marking papers for an extra half hour. When she stood to go home, her back was straighter, and her step lighter. She even hummed a little tune as she walked to her car.

NINETY MINUTES LATER, Nathaniel emerged from Mrs. Jacobson's house. Irma Jacobsen was in her seventies, widowed, and happy for the business, as there weren't many people interested in accordion lessons in the era of Madonna and Michael Jackson.

Nathaniel was so thin he nearly didn't cast a shadow, but he nonetheless lugged his heavy accordion case down the trail toward home. There were sidewalks between Mrs. Jacobson's house and home, but the trail was a shortcut, and what ten year old boy can resist a shortcut?

Ahead of Nathaniel, two other boys sat on their haunches, looking down into a stream that moved so slowly, it might have been mistaken for a long, skinny pond.

"You see anything, Craig?"

A sandy-blond boy with a pug nose and freckles shook his head. "Nah. Bobby says there's bullfrogs everywhere along here, but I think he's full of shit."

The second boy, stocky and dressed in a dirty t-shirt and jeans, got bored searching for frogs and looked up the trail. He nudged Craig, who squinted and said, "What's he carrying? It's bigger than he is."

The second boy said, "I think it's an accordion case. He takes lessons."

Craig looked at him like he had two heads. "Shut up, Wemmer. No one cares. Accordion lessons." He snorted. "If that's not asking to get beat up, I don't know what is."

Wemmer shut up.

"Come on. Let's have some fun."

Nathaniel looked ahead and saw the boys coming toward him, but he kept on at the same steady pace. Eventually, he stood right in front of Craig and Wemmer, who blocked his path. Nathaniel took the opportunity to set the heavy case down with a small sigh of relief. He grinned at the boys. "Hello."

"Hello," Craig said, mocking Nathaniel's adult-sounding way of talking. Craig was a talented mimic, which he used as both self-defense and as a vicious attack. "Hello," he repeated in the same tone, then looked at his friend expectantly.

Wemmer laughed appropriately. But he was surprised when even Nathaniel laughed.

"What the hell's wrong with you, Moon Pie?" This was a nickname he had hung on Nathaniel earlier in the year, but it had not gained as much traction as he would have liked.

Nathaniel gave the question some consideration. "Glad to say there's nothing at all wrong."

"Well, there's gonna be somethin' wrong. What's in the case?"

"It's an accordion."

Wemmer nodded wisely. "I knew that," he said quietly.

Craig shot him a look out of the corner of his eye. "Dude, it's 1989. No one plays the damned accordion, unless they just want to get their ass handed to them."

Nathaniel looked at Craig with a confused look and replied, "I disagree. I play one, and I don't want that."

Wemmer laughed again, but this time, it was *with* Nathaniel, not *at* him. Craig flushed red, took a step back, and threw an elbow up into Wemmer's mid-section. The "oof" that came out of him cut off any further laughter.

"So, you're a smart ass, huh?"

"I don't mean to be. I do have to head home now, though, my Aunt Andi is waiting for me."

"My Aunt Andi is waiting for me," Craig mimicked.

Nathaniel didn't react to the mocking, but just reached down to pick up his heavy case. As he did, Craig put both hands on his shoulders and shoved hard.

Nathaniel stumbled backwards three steps, then four, and pinwheeled his arms as his feet reached the small bank that ran along the edge of the creek. He eventually lost the battle with gravity and plunked butt-first into the creek, splashing dirty water everywhere. As he fell, he glanced at the accordion case to make sure that it was still safe.

Clothes will wash. I will wash. But Mom can't afford another accordion.

He picked himself up, wiped his hands on the front of his shirt, and stepped up on the bank.

"Whatcha gonna do now? You gonna cry?"

Nathaniel looked at him levelly. "Nothing to cry about. Just a little water. I do feel bad for you though."

Craig laughed. "You feel bad for *me?* I'm not the one dripping wet and about to go into the drink again." Craig took two steps toward Nathaniel when an old bicycle blurred in from the side, skidding to a halt and scattering gravel on him.

Craig jumped back in surprise. When he saw who was on the bike, his eyes widened. "Jesus, West, you almost hit me. What the hell?"

The boy on the bike wore his blondish hair in straight bangs, and even though he was only eleven, he had wisps of future sideburns already growing. He leaned forward on the rusted handlebars. He squinted one eye closed and said, "What's this kid ever done to you?"

"He bugs me."

"Because he's not an asshole? Because he's different?"

It was obvious that Craig had never considered *why* anyone deserved to have their ass kicked. If they had an ass, and they weren't one of his friends, he kicked it. He was simply playing his role in the ecosystem.

"Whatever, West, you're a weirdo, too." He backed away, out of range of Jon's long arms as he said that, just in case. He turned to Wemmer. "Let's blow. It stinks around here."

West continued to lean forward on his handlebars for a minute while he and Nathaniel watched the boys retreat.

Finally, he swung off the bike, let it drop, and took three strides to where Nathaniel stood, still dripping muddy water on the ground. He extended a hand.

Chapter Fourteen

Nathaniel shook Jon's hand and said, "Nathaniel Moon. Thank you. It would have been all right. He might have pushed me in a few times, but I don't think he would have done much worse than that. Still, it's nice not being any wetter than I am."

"I think I might need to teach you some self-defense, so people don't push you around like that."

"I guess it would be fun to learn, but I'm not going to fight. That's just not my way."

"Uh huh. Okay. Can you ride a bike?" Jon asked.

Nathaniel smiled, but shook his head. "Nope. Always wanted to learn, but haven't yet. Mom gave me the choice of a bike or that," he pointed to the accordion case, "for my last birthday. Can't have everything."

"Not sure you made the right choice there. Just curious, but why in the world did you decide you want to play the accordion? Are you a big Weird Al Yankovic fan?"

"No. Pretty big Frankie Yankovic fan, though."

"Who?"

"Frankie Yankovic was a great accordion player, but he's not related to Weird Al, even though they share the same last name. Kind of a weird coinkeedink, right? I like both of them, honestly but ..." Nathaniel noticed Jon's eyes were beginning to glaze over. He had often seen this happen when he talked about polka music, which was an inadvertent tagalong with some of the other memories he had brought forward. "Never mind. I don't know why, really." Nathaniel got a far-away look in his eyes. "I saw an accordion player on TV a few years ago, and I knew right then that I wanted to learn to play it, too. There's just something about the way all parts of it work in harmony together that makes me happy."

"That's pretty weird." Jon shrugged his shoulders.

"There's a lot of weird things about me," Nathaniel said.

"Me too," Jon said quietly. "Someday I'll tell you about some of the weird stuff that's happened to me."

"I'd like to hear it. I am a collector of weird and wonderful experiences."

"I know a joke about accordions. Wanna hear it?"

Nathaniel's eyes lit up. "Yes!"

"A local band had an accordion player. One night, after a gig, they stopped for dinner at a little café. They had just sat down and were getting ready to order when the accordion player slapped his forehead—you know, like those guys in the V-8 commercials?"

Nathaniel nodded, looking like he was ready to laugh at the punchline before he even heard it.

"The guy says, 'Uh-oh, I forgot to lock the car,' jumps up from the table and runs out to where his accordion was. He opens the door, and looks in, but it was too late. Somebody had already left two more accordions."

Nathaniel laughed as though that was the funniest joke he had ever heard.

"Mental note," Jon said, "Nathaniel Moon really likes stupid jokes."

"I do! Do you want me to tell you one?"

Jon shook his head. "No, not really. Look. You climb on the bike. I'll hold onto the handlebar and make sure you don't fall."

"But, my accordion—"

"I've got it." Jon leaned over and effortlessly picked up the case. He held the bike out to Nathaniel, who climbed on with a grin.

BY THE TIME THE BOYS arrived at Nathaniel's house, they had already discovered that, aside from their differences about the accordion, they both loved all three Indiana Jones movies and the Simpsons. As they walked the bicycle up the driveway that ran beside the house, they were showing off their impressions of various characters. Nathaniel did a passable Marge, but the best Jon could muster was Homer's "'Doh!"

He swung his leg off the bike. "Thanks for letting me kinda ride it. That was fun. You want to come in and meet my Aunt Andi? I know she'll want to meet you."

Nathaniel reached for his accordion, but Jon said, "I got it. Sure. Let's go in."

Nathaniel ran up the stairs and burst through the door. "Andi! I'm home!"

"Well, it's about time, mister," she said, coming around the corner from her bedroom. "Did you take the long way ..." She stopped short when she saw Nathaniel's dripping wet pants, shoes, and jacket, not to mention the hulking boy standing behind him. "Oh! What happened?" She cast a suspicious glare at Jon, ready to go into attack mode if needed.

"Oh, not much. Some kids wanted to make fun of me because of the accordion, Jon came along and stopped them. Oh. By the way, this is Jon." Nathaniel slipped his shoes off.

"Doesn't look like he stopped them to me. You're soaked. Go get changed, right now. Put your play clothes on."

Nathaniel ran toward his room, wet socks leaving damp footprints on the wood floor behind him.

Andi sized up the man-child who had apparently rescued Nathaniel from further dunkings. She smiled and said, "Nice to meet you, Jon. You managed to avoid the water?"

Jon smiled and nodded. "He wasn't big enough to push me in." He looked at Andi and said, "Georgia?"

Andi was used to people picking up on her accent, but not children, even over-sized ones.

"No, Arkansas. Still obvious, huh?"

Jon shrugged. "Not really. I just like accents, that's all."

Andi chuckled. "Why do I have a hunch you and Nathaniel are going to hit it off?

The door opened behind Jon and Violet came in, lugging a raincoat, a purse, and a yellow bag emblazoned with the logo of the local Mexican takeout. She entered talking. "...don't know why I ever trust the weatherman around here. He ..." She saw Jon and said, "Oh, sorry, I didn't know Andi was having friends over."

Jon looked a little embarrassed, but Andi said, "No, no, this is Jon. He's a friend of Nathaniel's. It looks like he saved Nathaniel from being bullied on the way home."

"Bullied again?" Violet sized Jon up, smiled, and said, "Well, fine. Thank you. Can I reward you with an enchilada or a," she rustled through the yellow bag, "a bean burrito?"

"Thanks, but no, my mom's got dinner waiting for me at home. I better go."

"Thanks for saving Nathaniel," both Violet and Andi said together, as though they had said it many times before.

"No problem." He looked at them seriously. "He's a cool kid."

Chapter Fifteen

Nathaniel's odd family unit was nearly complete—mother Violet, once-babysitter-now-Aunt Andi, and best friend Jon. The only thing needed to complete the picture of domesticity was a huge, slobbering furball, which, coincidentally, was exactly what Nathaniel and Jon found one day a few months later, as they walked home from school. Jon had started leaving his bike at home so they both could walk home together.

They rarely took the direct route home, but instead wandered whichever way their feet took them. Topics of conversation ranged from Nathaniel's observations on the human condition, which were met mostly with nods from Jon, to in-depth analysis on whether the Seattle Mariners would ever field a .500 team. The team had never managed it in their decade plus of existence, but since Nathaniel loved to root for the underdogs, the M's were the perfect choice as his favorite team.

They walked down Dover Street, a mixed-use area that ran parallel to the main drag through Middle Falls. The boys were walking past an alley that was lined with several dumpsters when they heard a "woof" and the thumping of large feet toward them. They peered into the darkness of the alley and saw an astonishing creature. Not a dog, exactly, but something more like an easy chair crossed with a mop. There were likely eyes buried under the long, floppy fur, but they couldn't be seen. The left ear pointed skyward and the right straight ahead. A magnificent tongue wagged from one side to the other with each bound of the animal.

Jon took a half-step forward and laid an arm across Nathaniel's chest, as a parent might do when braking in a car. The protection was unnecessary, though, as the lumbering animal skidded to a stop directly in front of them, sat on its rear haunches, and looked at them. Its expression seemed to say, *I thought you guys would never get here. I've been waiting forever.*

"That is the funniest looking dog I've ever seen," Jon said.

"Yeah," Nathaniel agreed. "Ain't he something? He's beautiful."

Jon looked at him, slightly askew. "Something, all right, but I'm not sure what. Come on, let's head for your house."

"Sure, sure. Just a minute." Nathaniel leaned down in front of the hairy beast and brushed the hair away from its eyes. "There you are." He patted the head and petted the neck, and the dog's tail thumped against the sidewalk. Finally, he put his head against its neck and buried his face in the matted fur.

"Nathaniel. You're grossing me out. God only knows where that dog has been. I can smell it from here."

"Yeah. It smells pretty bad. This is my dog, though."

"What? Oh, Andi and your mom are going to love that!"

"Not at first, but eventually they will. Let's go home."

Nathaniel turned toward home and set off at a steady trot. The dog padded along at his heels, as if on an invisible leash. Jon shook his head and followed along behind, muttering, "I gotta see this."

At home, Nathaniel threw the door open and led the parade into the living room. Violet was sitting on the couch reading, and looked up with a smile to welcome Nathaniel home. The smile froze on her face and slowly fell into a concerned frown when she saw the behemoth behind him.

"Well?" Nathaniel said.

This scene plays out a thousand times every day, across America and the world: a child brings a stray dog home, asks to keep it, and the parent says no. In most households, the child moans, begs and pleads, and the parent either relents and there's a new addition to the family, or doesn't, and there's an unhappy child until the scene plays itself out again sometime later.

The Moon household was not most households.

Violet looked at Nathaniel, then the slobbering, smelly dog behind him. Jon froze behind both of them, observing how the drama would play out.

Violet sighed, and said, "We need to have an understanding."

Nathaniel nodded, and as if replying by rote, said, "I'm responsible for the dog. I have to give him a bath every Saturday, and more often if he stinks, like he does now. I have to feed him, and walk him, and if he makes a mess in the house, I have to clean it up. If he's not a good member of the family, and I can't control him, we'll have to find him a different home."

"Are you sure, Nathaniel, about this particular dog, though? If you have your heart set on a dog, we could go down to the Humane Society and see all the dogs there that need homes. I'm sure there are some, umm, smaller dogs there. This one is a behemoth."

Nathaniel laid his hand on the dog's head, who repaid him by slathering the hand in saliva. "You're right, Mom. There are. And I know a smaller dog would be easier, and they all need homes too. But, we can't save all the dogs, just one." He looked happily at the mountain of fur beside him. "This is the one for us."

Andi walked in, carrying a mug of tea. She noticed the immense dog in the middle of the room, and stopped, splashing hot tea over hand. This made her jerk and cry out in pain, which spilled more hot tea on her, which made her drop the mug onto the hardwood floor, where it shattered into a dozen pieces.

"Sorry, Andi," Nathaniel said, then looked at his mom. "I'll go get a towel and clean that up, but I don't think it should count against Brutus."

Violet started to giggle. "Oh, my God. Really, Nathaniel? 'Brutus?'"

"It's his name."

An hour later, Jon and Nathaniel had managed to bathe Brutus, which was an adventure in itself. He didn't fight going into the bathtub, exactly, but he didn't help, either. By the time they got him wet and lathered up, the two boys were both as wet as the dog. When they unplugged the drain, the bottom of the tub was covered in yellowish-white clumps of fur.

"I think from now on, when I give him a bath, I'm just going to change into my swimsuit," Nathaniel said.

After he was allowed out of the tub, Brutus gave a shake that threw water over the entire bathroom, floor to ceiling, drenching the boys yet again. After they toweled him off, Andi and Violet appeared with brushes, combs, and clippers.

Andi had taken hairdressing classes at the community college, so she took the lead in the operation. They spent more than an hour rotating around Brutus like he was an Indy car pulled in for a pit stop. Andi clipped the matted fur where it couldn't be combed out, while Violet and the boys brushed at the sections they thought could be saved. Through it all, Brutus stood, tongue lolling, patiently waiting for a better part of his life to begin.

In the end, Brutus once again resembled a dog, if still a giant, homely dog who would never be beautiful. With a single exception: once the matted fur was removed from his face, two lovely, soulful brown eyes looked out at the world. It was hard to look into those eyes and not love him.

CYRUS CREECH SPUN HIS chair around and looked out his office window. Creech Coat and Uniform Manufacturing had undergone many changes over the previous six years. He had closed the original factory in Tubal and moved his family north, closer to Little Rock. His business had expanded and exploded during that time, and he was now the CEO of a much larger concern.

The growing business didn't mean he had forgotten about Nathaniel, however. Creech still thought about him every day, and his frustration grew with each passing month and year. He had fired J.R. when no noticeable results had resulted in the first twelve months, and was now working with a fourth agency trying to locate Nathaniel and his mother.

"It's almost 1990!" he screamed into the phone at the last report. "People don't just disappear. They're out there, and I will find them."

The investigation and search for Vivian and Nathaniel Hanrahan had cost Cyrus more than a small fortune, but with the success of his busines, he hadn't even noticed the drain. He continued to write out checks each month while pursuing each new angle, idea, or lead. He had thought the investigators were closing in on them twice, once in Durango, Colorado, and once in Oceanside, California. Both turned out to be false alarms.

Cyrus's attitude toward both Vivian and Nathaniel had also evolved over the years. Once he had believed that Nathaniel's gifts came directly from God and should be used for His glory. But the longer he was frustrated in finding them, the more he ascribed negative connotations to Nathaniel and his strange talent.

"Perhaps it wasn't from the glory of God, after all," he would say. And, "If he were truly of God, he would share his miracles with the world." And, "Somewhere, he no doubt bears the Mark of the Beast."

These were Creech's words and thoughts on the surface. But deeper, where the truth of his life was, it was simply frustration at his inability to find them, and, most importantly, to a man who seemed to have total control in his life, the fact that he could not control them.

Chapter Sixteen
1995

For the next six years, things ran as smoothly for Nathaniel, Andi, Violet, and Brutus as they ever did for any family. There were minor blips, of course. Andi had a hard time holding a job long term, because she hated being away from home each day. Her heart was in being a homemaker, and she always managed to find a way to make that happen, again and again. Violet was once again rising through the ranks at her job, though, so they didn't really need Andi's income to get by.

Nathaniel lost interest in his studies sometime during his freshman year in high school, and brought home a semester report card with two "C's" and a "D" on it. Violet was flabbergasted. Nathaniel so often did unusual things, but they were more in line with floating a few inches off the bed when he slept, or astutely cutting to the heart of a debate with a few quiet words, as opposed to failing tests.

When Violet asked him why he brought home such a poor report card after ten years of exemplary ones, Nathaniel was honest, but that was not surprising. He seemed incapable of lying—not the outright lie, or a lie by omission or partial truth, or even the always-popular white lie, designed to save someone's feelings. However, Violet had told him that when he was older and his wife or girlfriend asked him if he liked her haircut, or if her jeans made her butt look big, the only two correct answers were, respectively, "Yes, I love it," and "No, not at all." Nathaniel had filed these instructions away with a marker to remind him of when to use them.

So, when Violet asked him about the report card, he said, "Because I didn't care, what we were studying was too simple and boring, and I just decided not to do the work."

"But, we want to have all options open for you, when you are ready to go to college, so you need to get good grades the rest of the way."

"I've decided I don't want to go to college. I've spent too much time sitting in a classroom already. I'll finish high school, and I'll get good grades, because it's important to you, but I'm not going on to college. The job I want to do won't require a degree. Just empathy and a strong back."

Vivian contemplated asking him what that job would be, because she knew he would tell her, but decided to leave that question for another day. Nathaniel had taught her many things by example, one of which was, *Don't borrow trouble. It will find you if it must.*

Beyond these small blips, life proceeded apace. As soon as they had arrived in Middle Falls, Violet had found a job as a receptionist at a medical center. Nine years later, she had worked her way up to Assistant Director, and, if you asked anyone who worked there, they would tell you that they went to Violet first with every problem.

On Halloween night, 1995, the smooth path they had enjoyed for years became twisted and bumpy.

Nathaniel was sixteen, Jon had just turned seventeen, and both were too old to go trick-or-treating. Violet had asked them to stay home and watch Jamie Lee Curtis scream her way through *Halloween,* but the boys weren't interested in that, either. Watching that movie on that night was a tradition for Violet and Andi, but this year, Andi was saving up for a new stereo and so had one of her intermittent jobs—delivering for *The Leaning Tower of Pizza.*

Jon and Nathaniel decided to walk around town and see what they could see, although they didn't put a lot of effort into their costumes. Nathaniel found a long blond wig and a pair of black-framed glasses, Jon tucked his hair behind his ears and found a Wayne's World baseball cap, and they transformed themselves into Garth and Wayne. Of course, the real Wayne wasn't a hulking six-foot three-inch, 225-pound teenager, but Nathaniel had been working on his mimicry, and he had Garth down pretty well.

More than anything, they just wanted to be out and about, watching the kids trick-or-treat, stopping by Sammy's Corner Grocery for a Coke and a bag of Twizzlers, and hanging out with each other. The highlight of their night was when they saw four guys dressed as KISS. They bowed repeatedly, repeating "We're not worthy," and cracking themselves up. Eventually, they tired of the limited fun a small town Halloween could offer, and headed back to Nathaniel's house. Andi had promised to bring a giant pizza home with her at the end of her shift.

"We're too early," Jon said, nodding at the driveway at Nathaniel's house. Violet's Toyota Camry was there, but Andi's older-model Mazda was not.

Nathaniel shrugged and hurried up the steps. "Well, hopefully, we stayed gone long enough that Mom has watched her movie. Maybe we can find *Night of the Living Dead* on until Andi gets here."

Nathaniel threw open the door and would have been bowled over by the attack from Brutus if Jon hadn't been standing at the ready, bracing his shoulders.

"Sorry, boy. This just wasn't a good night to be walking around with a giant, shaggy dog. You would have taken all the attention away from our awesome costumes. Hey, Mom," he said, plopping down on the couch, "Where's Andi and the pizza? We've only had dinner and a bunch of candy and pop while we were out. We're growing boys!"

The phone rang, and Violet said, "She was supposed to get off half an hour ago. I'll bet she had to make some late deliveries, and that's her."

"I've got it," Nathaniel said, sliding across the kitchen floor in his stocking feet. He picked up the cordless phone, extending the antenna in one smooth motion. "Hello, Moon residence." The smile faded from his face. A short pause, then, "Mom? It's the hospital. They're asking for you."

Violet vaulted up off the couch and was across the room in two seconds. "Hello?" She listened intently, then said, "We're on our way."

She dropped the phone, clattering, onto the counter. "Shoes on. Andi's been in an accident. Let's go."

Chapter Seventeen

Jon left for home and let the Moons go to the hospital alone. As much as he was part of the family, Violet's expression told him that she wanted it to be just her and Nathaniel.

In the car on the short ride across town to the hospital, Violet was quiet, and focused on driving. When they pulled into the Emergency Room parking lot, she turned the engine off, but didn't immediately open the door.

Looking straight ahead, she said, "They didn't tell me how bad it is, but from their tone, I'm afraid it might be serious. I'm hoping she's just got a broken bone or two, and we can take her home soon to heal up. But prepare yourself for something more than that."

Nathaniel nodded, laid his hand on the door handle.

Then let's go.

Violet reached out and touched his shoulder, holding him back.

"When you were just a little boy, I asked you to not use what's inside you—to not heal anyone, unless we talked about it."

And I haven't, at least, not much, and things have been good. You were right.

"Mom. You don't have to say anything. I know. If Andi is in bad shape, I will help her."

"You haven't done it in so long, I was afraid you would have forgotten it, or couldn't do it."

When you say things like that, I know you truly don't understand this, but that's okay. You don't need to.

"It would be easier to forget how to breathe."

"Sometimes I wonder if I was wrong. I was afraid. You are so special, I've been afraid that someone would try to take you away from us."

"It's okay. If it was something I really wanted to do, I would have just talked to you about it. But, I just want to be what I've been—a normal kid, living a normal life. If I had helped every person that was sick, that life would have been over pretty quick."

"Now that I hear you say that, I feel selfish for worrying about it. But, let's worry about that later, honey. Let's go and make sure our Andi is okay."

They hurried into the ER entrance and to the admissions desk.

"Can you tell me what room Andrea Moon is in?"

The woman at the desk consulted a computer monitor, then said, "106, just down the hall on the left."

Violet and Nathaniel hurried down the hall, checking the numbers on each door. When they spotted Room 106, there was a doctor wearing a white lab coat and talking to a nurse, who was holding a chart and making notes. When Violet tried to push past them, the doctor held up a hand to stop them.

"Can I help you?"

"I'm Violet Moon. I'm looking for my sister, Andi." The practiced lie slipped easily off her tongue.

The nurse melted away, but the doctor reached out and touched Violet's elbow. He indicated a small waiting room. "Let's sit down over here, so we can talk."

Violet opened her mouth to object, but Nathaniel said, "Mom, he probably has the answers we need," and they followed the doctor to a small semi-circle of chairs.

"I'm very sorry to say..."

As soon as Nathaniel heard those words, he looked up at the ceiling and closed his eyes. He calmed his heart rate and breathing. When he opened them again, the doctor was saying, "We did absolutely everything we could to resuscitate her, but she was already gone when they brought her in."

Violet's head dropped. When she looked up, her face was wet with tears, but a cunning look played across her face.

"Doctor, is there any way we can see her, spend a few minutes with her? She's our only family."

"Of course. We'll be moving her soon, but take whatever time you need with her." He stood, said, "I'm very sorry," and hurried on to other patients.

She pushed the door open and found the room as quiet as a tomb. All the machines and monitors had been turned off. A small lamp on a bedside table cast a feeble, yellowish glow. Andi lay in the bed. The wreck, while traumatic, had left her face clear and untroubled. For all the world, she appeared to be sleeping.

"Oh, Andi." Violet struggled for control. She looked to Nathaniel, eyes pleading. She said only two words: "Can you?"

Nathaniel, still a boy to all outward appearances, met her eyes and said, "I can, but, I don't know if I will."

"But, this is our Andi. Our dearest Andi."

Nathaniel smiled, a cheerful smile, and said, "Almost everyone is someone's dearest. Still, there are times they need to go, and we need to let them go. I remember that."

Violet nodded. "You'll know. I trust your judgment."

That's what she says. What she means is, she's sure I'll do what she wants.

Just an hour before, Nathaniel had been wearing a silly Halloween costume and cracking wise with Jon. Now he was asked to make a decision that went somewhere beyond the border of life and death.

He sat on the bed beside Andi, picked up her hand, and held it between his own. It was cool, but not yet cold. He closed his eyes and reached out for Andi. Initially, he saw and felt nothing but blackness, but then, in the far corner of his consciousness, he saw her. She was just a small glimmer of light at first, and she was so far away, but as he looked at her, Andi drew nearer.

Soon enough, she stood in front of him. She glowed with happiness and vitality.

"Hello, Andi."

She wrapped her arms around Nathaniel and kissed him on the cheek. "I've been lingering here, waiting for you, but it has been so hard. I am being pulled away, and I want to go."

"Of course. That is the way of it. Violet asked me to find you and bring you back."

"I knew you could bring me back to that life, but that's not why I waited for you. I was sorry I didn't say good-bye." She touched his cheek. "I love you. And you know I love Violet. I am so grateful I got to spend this time with you. You both brought me so much happiness. You are my true family, and I know we will see each other again. Will you tell Violet how much I love her, but that I chose to go on?"

"Of course. She knows how you feel. You've shown her every day, in all the small ways you took care of us. But, I will tell her."

Andi reached down, took both of Nathaniel's hands in hers. "Thank you for letting me go. If you had wanted me to, I would have stayed."

"I know. We'll hold the happy memories of you in our heart forever."

Andi let go and took a few tentative steps backward. Then she shot her hands straight up, giggled with happiness, and disappeared.

Nathaniel stayed where he was for an unknown time, cherishing Andi and her perfect spirit, then opened his eyes.

Violet had moved to sit on the bed as well, and sat looking back and forth at him, then Andi.

"She wanted me to tell you how much she loved you, and how happy our time together was, but she's gone now."

Violet turned to focus on Andi's empty body, as though she might have the ability to bring her back, where Nathaniel had failed. Finally, she turned her attention to Nathaniel.

"Why would she ever leave us?"

"Because," Nathaniel said simply, "it was time."

Chapter Eighteen
2018

Nathaniel was as good as his word. He had gotten straight "A's" for the rest of his high school years, and graduated a very respectable twenty-second out of his class of one hundred and seventy five. That was typical of Nathaniel—he enjoyed performing and excelling, but he much preferred to stay out of the spotlight.

Jon had to work much harder to get essentially the same grades, but he had never been afraid of hard work. He graduated just ahead of Nathaniel and that was good enough to get him accepted into the University of Oregon.

Victoria did her best to not compare Nathaniel's apparent lack of ambition to the more fired-up Jon, but she struggled with it. She knew that Nathaniel could accomplish absolutely anything he wanted, so when he told her that what he wanted was to be a janitor at Middle Falls hospital, she was crestfallen.

Nathaniel was steadfast in his desire to work at the hospital, though, and over time, Victoria had come to accept that it was a place where he could accomplish much good, while still living the non-headline grabbing life he had chosen.

In 2002, Jon had returned from the University of Oregon with not only a Bachelor of Architecture, but, much more importantly, a new bride. He and Melissa had met during his second year, and fallen in love during his third year. They got married back in Middle Falls over Christmas break, Jon's final year at the university. In 2010, they had a beautiful baby girl they named Kate, but everyone called her Katie. They asked Nathaniel to be her godfather, of course.

In the years that Jon was gone to college, he and Nathaniel stayed as close as ever. Nathaniel drove to Eugene for big football games, and Jon came back to Middle Falls every chance he got.

Nathaniel, meanwhile, continued to work the swing shift from three to midnight as the night janitor in the critical care wing of Middle Falls Hospital. Even though he didn't get home from work until after midnight on the nights he worked, Nathaniel was a habitually early riser, up before the sun most days. He needed very little sleep and loved spending hours in the recording studio he had built in the basement of his little house. His love of the accordion had given way first to the steel guitar, then acoustic guitar, and eventually various keyboards and drum kits. He had spent the last year trying to learn to drum like Max Roach, which is like picking up an electric guitar and trying to learn to play like Eric Clapton. He knew it wouldn't happen, but also knew it was more about the journey anyway.

Nathaniel composed music and recorded it on the sixteen-track mixing board he had bought second hand. Like the rest of the house, he and Jon had done all the work themselves, from soundproofing the walls to running the wiring and installing acoustical ceiling panels. It had only taken them a few years to get it the way Nathaniel wanted it. Now, he had a perfect little room where he could record by himself or with friends.

The music he made was a combination of jazz and new age, with the flavor of Mexican Polka thrown in somewhere. It was not commercial music, certainly, which didn't concern Nathaniel in any way. He recorded for himself, and piped the music upstairs, where it played whenever he was home. Visitors often had strong reactions to the music, ranging anywhere from a horrified expression to a few who were initially repelled but eventually gave in to its charms.

When faced with these reactions, Nathaniel would switch over to more mainstream Chilean flute music or the like, and say, "My music is an acquired taste, like anchovies. Except eventually, some people learn to love anchovies."

Nathaniel had a few life mottos. Chief among them was, "What other people think of me is none of my business." Another was, "What is right, and what is easy, are rarely the same thing." The one he had written on a piece of cardboard and stuck above his mixing board said, "Everything is impossible, until you see someone do it."

Nathaniel lived several miles outside the city limits of Middle Falls, on a small plot of land that had been created as a flag lot when several other plats of land had been subdivided. That gave him the advantage of having a smaller, less expensive piece of land that was surrounded by twenty acre parcels on all sides. His nearest neighbors were a quarter mile away in any direction, which gave him the privacy he cherished.

Nathaniel had bought the land on a contract when he was just a year out of high school. However, he had continued to live at home with Violet for two years after graduating so he could pour all his modest salary from the hospital into getting the land paid off as quickly as possible. As soon as he managed that, he bought an old travel trailer, dropped it on the property, and moved in.

As soon as Jon got back from U of O, he went to work for a small architectural firm in Middle Falls during the day, and he and Nathaniel designed the house that would eventually go on the property. They spent many nights in Jon's small apartment, talking and dreaming over the plans, while Melissa occasionally brought the woman's perspective to the proceedings, which was much-needed.

Nathaniel lived in the travel trailer for five years, and grew most of his own food in the rich soil behind the site of his future house. During those years, Nathaniel saved his money. His goal was to be able to build the house, including all the improvements to the land, and own it free and clear the day it was completed.

Nathaniel would have been content continuing to live in the travel trailer, but he had to admit that when you owned a dog the size of Brutus, a little more space was more than a luxury. When Brutus laid down in the middle of the floor of the tiny trailer, Nathaniel had to resort to elaborate gymnastic maneuvers to get around him.

Not to mention that it was getting more and more difficult for Brutus to get up the tiny metal steps into the travel trailer. Because of the way Nathaniel had found Brutus, he had no way to know how old the dog was, but by 1999, he knew that Brutus was at least eleven years old, and almost certainly older. He noticed that Brutus was moving slower, his joints were stiffer, and his eyesight was failing. Every dog lover knows and dreads the pattern of a dog's life—that eventually the suffering of the dog outweighs the potential grief at losing a companion.

But other dog lovers did not have the options that Nathaniel Moon did. When the day came that he knew Brutus was suffering, Nathaniel sat in the grass with him and laid a hand on top of his head. Brutus closed his eyes and laid his massive head on Nathaniel's knee. His trusting brown eyes looked into Nathaniel's.

Nathaniel couldn't talk to Brutus, of course—he wasn't Dr. Doolittle—but he did what he could to communicate with him. *What do you want, my constant friend? For me to make you young again, or to be released to whatever is next for you? You have been such a positive presence in my life. I would miss you if you were gone, but I want to do what's best for you. For your mighty spirit.*

It would seem that having the power to deny death and restore health would be a wonderful gift, but Nathaniel knew the truth of it. Long-extended life, even a pain-free life, was not always desired, and the Law of Unintended Consequences always raised its head. He had vowed to never extend the life of anyone or anything without knowing if that was what they wished.

They sat together for long, silent minutes, soaking up the sunshine, Nathaniel stroking Brutus's ears and scratching between his eyes. Five minutes later, they both stood, but this time Brutus's joints were no longer stiff, and his rheumy eyes had cleared. He put his head down between his feet, shook his head, and woofed like he hadn't done in years.

When Nathaniel had "fixed" Pup Spitton years before, he was too young to know, but whoever or whatever Nathaniel fixed, stayed fixed. So it was with Brutus, who would never have so much as a touch of arthritis for the rest of his exceptionally long life. Now, so many years after they had first found each other, Brutus was as young and healthy as he had ever been—he still jumped up into Nathaniel's pickup truck when it was time to go for a drive, and he still spent happy hours fruitlessly chasing rabbits and squirrels behind the house.

From the road, Nathaniel's house looked modest, and it was, in many ways. Middle Falls was famous for having a high water table, so basements were rare, but the soil on Nathaniel's property drained well, so that had given him the perfect place for his dream musical studio. Above ground, the house was small—eleven hundred square feet, although it was only that big because Jon insisted on it. Left to his own devices, Nathaniel would have had a much smaller footprint.

"I know you could live in a space the size of the travel trailer, but eventually you might want to have a wife, and she's not going to want to live in a house the size of a closet. Besides, you need a second bedroom so that when your best friend crashes for the night, he doesn't have to sleep on the couch, or God forbid, a hide-a-bed."

Nathaniel laughed at the thought of his bulky best friend attempting to sleep on a hide-a-bed, with a metal bar firmly across his shoulders. He relented, and Jon designed him a lovely two-bedroom house with a great room concept built around a massive river rock fireplace and an A-frame window that looked out on the forested hills behind his house. The house was small, but the finishes and flat surfaces were straight out of *Property Brothers*.

The day Nathaniel and Jon packed the last of the tools away and vacuumed up the last of the sawdust, they sat on the patio on the back deck, and enjoyed the accomplishment of something they had built with their own hands. They each nursed a beer and watched the sun set behind the tree covered hill.

Nathaniel tipped his Budweiser toward Jon and said, "Thank you, brother, for everything you did. It's perfect. Without you, I would still be living in the travel trailer. Seems like you've been doing me favors since the first day I met you down at the creek. I owe you."

Jon nodded. "I'm sure I'll cash that all in someday, when one of your songs hits the Top 40."

They both laughed at that ludicrous idea.

Sitting in rickety lawn chairs, squinting into the setting sun, Jon took a long look at Nathaniel and said, "There's something I've been meaning to tell you all these years. I almost told you that very first day, when you got dunked in the creek, but I didn't, and then I just never knew how to bring it up. Today, putting the finishing touches on your house, seems like the time. Are you up for an unbelievable story?"

.

Chapter Nineteen

J on took a long drag on his beer, crumpled the can, and fished another out of the cooler that sat between them. Nathaniel sat quietly, staring out at the hills.

"This isn't my first lifetime."

I don't think this is the first lifetime for any of us, Jon.

"My first life was both the same, and completely different, if that makes sense. I mean, I was born here in Middle Falls, and everything was the same—same parents, same friends growing up, everything. Except in that life, I played sports. A lot. In high school, I played basketball, baseball, football and track. Sometimes I had to run straight from a track meet to a baseball game. I loved that."

He cracked the beer open with a satisfying *psssht* sound.

"The University of Oregon recruited me, but told me they wanted me to concentrate on football, so I gave up everything else. I went to Oregon then, just like I did in this life, but I didn't study architecture, I mostly studied how to be a big man on campus while taking the easiest classes I could find."

Jon was silent for a moment, reflecting.

"I'll be honest. I wasn't a very good dude. Too much success, too early, went to my head, and I was pretty certain my feces were of the non-smelly variety, if you know what I mean."

Nathaniel smiled and nodded in understanding.

"I got drafted by the Oakland Raiders to play middle linebacker. I wasn't one of those first round draft picks, but I still got enough money to do whatever I wanted, I guess. Problem was, I couldn't really think of anything I did want. I never got married, never had kids." He shook his head. "I can't even imagine life without Melissa and Katie. That's probably why I'm not rich, but I am happy in this life, instead of having more money than sense in that one. Anyway, back then, we didn't know much about concussions and brain injuries and CTE. Not like we know now."

Unconsciously, Jon ran his fingers through his close-cropped hair, as if feeling the impact of some of those blows across the lifetimes.

"I had five concussions, or maybe I should say five *registered* concussions. A lot of times, we just called it *getting your bell rung* or a *stinger*. Whatever you want to call them, they added up, and they did something to me. Before I was even out of football, I was having trouble remembering defensive formations. Two years after I retired, I had to write down my address, in case I couldn't find my way home. That's bad enough, but there were worse things. I was angry all the time. I lashed out at everyone, but mostly, anybody that tried to get close to me. One day, I raised my hand to hit my girlfriend, and that was it. The look on her face stopped me, thank God."

He drained off half the fresh beer in one long pull.

"I went straight home, typed up my suicide note, donating my brain to study the effects of all those concussions, then put a gun to my chest and pulled the trigger. Here's how lost I was: as I lay there on my bed, about to pull the trigger to kill myself, all I could think about was whether ESPN would interrupt their programming to announce I'd done it, or if it would just be a throwaway at the end of Sportscenter." Jon chuckled a little, but it was a bitter, tinny laugh. "You'd think that would be the end of it, right? I should have gone on to whatever's next?"

"You would think," Nathaniel said.

"But I didn't. The next thing I knew, I felt like I was falling. Here's the weird part. My *mom* reached out and caught me to keep from falling on my face. My mom, who had died almost ten years before me. We were walking through the Safeway parking lot, and she reached out and caught me like it was no big deal, like I had been there the whole time. It was like my whole life was given a do-over. It took me a while to wrap my head around it, I'll admit. Eventually, I figured out that I had been given a second chance, although I have no idea why."

He turned and looked at Nathaniel.

"Thirty years later, I still don't understand any of it. But, when I came to in my ten year old body, everything that had been wrong with me was gone. No more headaches, or uncontrollable anger. It really was a second chance. So, I decided a couple of things. First, I would never step on a football field again. Second, I would try to make up for what a jerk I was by stopping bullying every chance I got."

Jon smiled. "That's where you came into the picture. I didn't remember you at all from my first life, but when I went back to school, I saw you everywhere, and you were always being so cool with people, and people went out of their way to bully you. You never fought back, but you never let them get to you, either. I decided whatever you had, that's what I wanted. I saw my chance when Craig pushed you down in Miller's Creek that day. Sorry I didn't get there quite in time."

Nathaniel grinned at the memory. "No problem. It was a good beginning for us."

"I always figured that maybe the same thing had happened to you—that you had just lived this life so many times that you had everything figured out."

"Do I have everything figured out? Doesn't feel like it most days."

"Well, you certainly do more than I, or anybody else I know, does."

"No, I am not living the same life over and over." Nathaniel paused and thought back over the many lives he had lived. "I've only lived each life once. It just shows you how many different ways things are done in our universe. We are all spiritual beings, having a human experience, but doing so in different ways. I'm sure that's a metaphor for something, if I wanted to think about it."

"So, how come you are the way you are? I've never known anyone like you."

"Before I was even born, I decided to bring some of the memories with me into this world. When I was a little boy, I used some of those memories to save a man's life. Then, I did it again, and stopped a boy from dying. That didn't turn out so well. We got some unwanted attention and made a run for it. That's how we came to Middle Falls. After that, Mom asked me to not do it, so we didn't have to run again." He drained the rest of the beer and set it down on the deck. "It's made for an interesting life so far. A constant tightrope walk, wanting to use what I can do to help people, while still wanting to be left alone to live the life I want to live. Sometimes, it feels selfish, but I do what I can to help people."

"Not just people," Jon said, pointedly looking at Brutus, at least thirty years old with the energy of a pup.

Nathaniel nodded in agreement. "Not just people. Change is coming, though. I know it. Eventually, I'm going to fall off this tightrope, and I have no idea if there's a net below or not."

Chapter Twenty

Nathaniel Moon pushed a wide broom down a side hallway of Middle Falls Hospital. It was a little after 8:00 p.m., and he had four hours left on his shift. Nathaniel's mind was as quiet as the patients who lay asleep in the beds in the Critical Care Unit. His broom whispered over the linoleum floor in a pattern he had traced thousands of times.

Nathaniel glanced into Room 3218. An old man lay awake, staring at the ceiling, drawing one labored breath after another. His mouth was open, and each breath sounded like the wind whistling through a forest in winter.

Nathaniel paused, almost imperceptibly, and reached into the room with his mind.

As good a place as any.

Nathaniel returned to his pushcart, retrieved the dustpan and collected the dirt that had tracked in on people's feet in the last 24 hours. He pushed his cart into the janitor's closet at the end of the hall, retrieved his brown bag lunch, and returned to Room 3218.

When he walked in, there was a nurse bustling around the room. "Can I help you?"

"Hello, you must be Shelley, the new nurse. I'm Nathaniel."

"Ahhh, the famous Nathaniel. I think I heard more about you than I did anything else in my training."

"I'm just the night janitor, but I often spend my lunch hour in with the critical care patients, if they don't have any other visitors."

"So I hear. It's a bit unusual, allowing non-family members as visitors at night, isn't it?"

"I suppose. I've been doing it for years. For many, this wing is their final stop, and I hate to see them alone, with no visitors, so I do what I can."

"Right. That's the word I got. One of the nurses said you're better with the patients than all the doctors in the hospital put together. That you're some kind of miracle worker."

"Oh, no, not at all. As I said, I'm just a janitor."

She smiled and shook her head. "Everyone here knows you're more than that, and from the way they talk about you, everyone loves you for it."

Nathaniel smiled but changed the subject away from himself. "That's always good to hear, isn't it? So what is this gentleman's name?"

"This is Mr. Isaac Donelly. I'm not sure how much company he will be for you. He hasn't spoken a word since they brought him in. He just stares at the ceiling, or sleeps."

"There's nothing wrong with keeping your own counsel. If more people did, the world would be a happier place, don't you think?"

Shelley stopped, thought for a moment, and finally said, "You're right, you're right." She bustled out of the room chuckling slightly to herself. "You're a strange one, Mr. Moon."

Nathaniel sat in the chair next to the bed and unrolled the brown bag in his lap. He was a light eater, and tonight he had a container of brown rice that he had sprinkled some Sriracha sauce over.

He spooned rice into his mouth and chewed contemplatively. A moment later, he said, "Good evening, Mr. Donelly. How are you, sir?"

Mr. Donelly, who, other than blinking, hadn't moved in more than twelve hours, turned his head to stare at Nathaniel. He closed his mouth with a wet slap, but his wheezing breath continued unchanged. After many long seconds of contemplation, he said, "I'm goddamn dying here, aren't I? What's it to you?"

Nathaniel dabbed at his mouth with a paper towel.

Isaac Donelly peered closer at Nathaniel, taking in his dark wavy hair and the gray work shirt that had his name stitched over the pocket.

"You the custodian or something?"

"I am," Nathaniel agreed.

"No way to run a hospital, I'll tell you. Having the custodial staff harassing the patients."

"What did you do for a living, Mr. Donelly?"

"I was a photographer."

Nathaniel waited patiently. He had drawn out thousands of these conversations over the years, and knew the virtue of patience.

"Not one of those fancy, 'take a picture of a mountain and pretend it's art' kind of photographers, either. I owned my own shop, then worked for Sears for twenty years, working with the same crummy backgrounds over and over, trying to get the same bratty kids to smile."

Nathaniel nodded, but still didn't speak.

"Lost that job in '91, though." His eyes grew distant as he sorted through the memories he hadn't ordered in a long time. "Then I went to work for one of those car sales rags. Spent my days driving from one piddly-ass town to another, taking pictures of cars no one wanted. Say, my throat's awful dry. Can you help me get a drink of that water?"

Nathaniel set his container of rice aside and picked up the plastic glass of water. He held the straw so Donelly could drink.

The ghost of a smile crossed the old man's cracked lips. "Say, I didn't mean to sound so cross. You seem like a decent fellow."

That could be because I've barely spoken. We all seem more decent when we're not talking.

"Anyway," Mr. Isaac continued, "eventually those damn digital cameras came along and that job faded away, too. Now, I suppose, everyone just takes pictures of what they want to sell with their phones, don't they."

"They do, yes."

"Another good career gone. What are kids going to do when all the jobs are gone, or being done by robots?"

"Maybe they'll learn to build the robots."

"Until the damned robots learn to build themselves, then we'll all be in a hell of a jam, won't we?"

Nathaniel picked up the rice again and went back to eating his dinner.

"So, is this what you do? Just come and sit with people that are fixin' to die?"

"Yes."

"You're real, though, right? Flesh and blood, and I'm not imagining you."

"I'm every bit as real as you are."

Donelly raised his eyebrows at that. "Don't know how reassuring that is. I could've died an hour ago for all I know, and this is just the beginning of my eternal torment."

That made Nathaniel smile. "Is that what you think is next? Eternal torment?"

Donelly thrust his chin out in initial defiance, but thought better of it, and sadly said, "I suppose I do."

"Why?"

"I don't want to talk about it."

"That's fine. I understand. It's a sensitive subject." Nathaniel went back to his dinner and sat in companionable silence.

Finally, Donelly said, "It's my brother. I think I killed my brother."

"That's usually not something you have any doubt about—if you kill somebody, that is."

"We were partners. Donelly Brothers Photography. We didn't need cutesy names then. Things were more solid. We opened the business in '62. Things went fine, for a while, mostly because I was doing everything we needed to keep us afloat. If there was a wedding to shoot, or a family portrait, old Isaac was the man for the job. Otto always had his head in the clouds, wanting to shoot pretty landscapes that we could put up in our window."

Even more than fifty years later, he scoffed at the memory.

"I got tired of it. Who wouldn't? What did he expect? For me to keep doing all the heavy lifting, while he did all the artsy stuff that made the young girls swoon?"

Did young girls swoon at photos of sunsets and lakes? I suppose maybe they did.

Donelly cast a canny glance at Nathaniel to see if he was paying attention, judging him.

"In the end, I cut him out. He was terrible at paperwork, contracts. It wasn't hard to do. He was crap at the details. One day, when he strolled in, twenty minutes late, just like usual, he noticed that the name on the door had changed to just *Donelly Photography*. He never said a word. He just looked at me for a long time, standing behind the counter, looking right back at him, then he turned around and left."

"Unless you shot him as he left, you probably didn't kill him, then."

"Not right away, you're right. It was worse. I should have seen it. I needed him, and he needed me. I didn't understand it. I did all the real work, but once Otto left, the business disintegrated. I had to close the doors a year later. And Otto. He just drifted away."

"I'm willing to bet he didn't just disintegrate, though."

"You're right, he didn't, but even if he had I wouldn't have known or cared for a long time. I was busy trying to run the shop. Then after that closed, I had to find a job to pay the bills. I didn't think about Otto for years. Maybe ten years later, I ran into a classmate who had been friends with him. He told me Otto had died years earlier. He drank himself to death."

"And you blame yourself for that."

"Of course. If I hadn't taken the company from him, he wouldn't have ended up like that."

"Perhaps. We all make hundreds of decisions every day, and each one of them changes not only the rest of our lives, but the lives of countless others. We rarely take much responsibility for that unless we feel guilty."

Donelly turned his eyes away from Nathaniel and looked out the window into the darkness.

"I'm glad I'm dying. I'm tired of carrying this around. I hope Dante was wrong."

"How so?"

"I don't want to end up in some circle of Hell, lugging something heavy around, just like I've lugged this memory around in life."

"I don't blame you." Nathaniel finished his rice, wiped his mouth and put the container back in his brown bag.

Donelly looked at him suspiciously. "That's it? You're going back to sweeping floors now?"

"It's my job, so yes. Why?"

"I don't know why, but there's something about you. I thought I was going to tell you my troubles, and then you were going to tell me a parable or something that would make me feel better."

Nathaniel rested his hands on his knees. "Would you like me to tell you a parable?"

"God, no."

"There you are." Nathaniel smiled. "I do have some advice that might help you, but the worst advice in the world is the unwanted kind. Do you want to hear it?"

Isaac Donelly was not a man who had wanted or taken advice often in his life, but standing here, at the yawning precipice to whatever was next, he softened.

"I guess I would."

"Don't worry, it's painless. I won't tell you to let go of all this heaviness you've carried around for so many years. Instead, I'll tell you to think about your life as objectively as you can. Look honestly at what you did, and why. Think about the core reasons why you pushed your brother away. Then, plant a marker in your mind at the point you made that decision. That way, when you come to it again in your next life, you'll have a better chance to recognize a similar situation and make a different choice."

Nathaniel stood, stepped next to the bed, and put his hand out. Donelly hesitated, but eventually reached out his own hand, shaking with palsy. Nathaniel took it and held it. Immediately, the shaking passed. The wheeze of Donelly's breathing quieted, and the tension in his body eased.

"What did you do? I'm ready to go."

"No need to worry. I didn't stop that, just eased your way. It's hard to think when you are wracked by pain, or dulled by drugs, so I took that away."

Donelly's face, which had been a hard mask since Nathaniel had walked into the room, eased into a more human expression. Tears sprang to his eyes, and he grasped Nathaniel's hand fiercely.

"Thank you."

"Use this time wisely, Mr. Donelly."

Two minutes later, Nathaniel Moon was pushing his broom down the corridor, tracing a path he had traced thousands of times before.

Chapter Twenty-One

The next day, Nathaniel and Brutus set off from the back porch, headed straight for the foothills that marked the western boundary of his property. His neighbors, who owned the 100 acre parcel behind him, used that portion of their land as a privacy buffer to keep anyone else from building behind their home. They had given him permission to hike the hills any time he wanted, and on sunny days, he often took them up on their offer.

Nathaniel had filled out some over the years, but he would always be lanky, with long legs and arms that swung wide when he hiked. Brutus ran ahead of him, then back, then to the side, and then back. Where Nathaniel might hike three or four miles on one of their jaunts, Brutus likely ran ten. He slept very well on the nights after their outings.

There was a small, rough path that Nathaniel had worn to the foothills over the years. It wasn't straight, but wound its crooked way via the easiest passage. He and Brutus walked up the side of the first hill and down the other, with Nathaniel humming a musical idea that had come to him the night before. Brutus pointedly ignored his humming, as he shared the same opinion of Nathaniel's music that the rest of the world held.

Once they crested the hill, there was a short descent into a small valley that ran as a channel before another hill. They descended the trail to a year-round stream. It was small, but Nathaniel often saw trout and even the occasional salmon swimming in it. When they arrived at the stream, Nathaniel laid on his belly and drank his fill of the cold water, while Brutus did the same, somewhat more noisily.

He looked around, picked out a solid looking fir tree with a level area around it, and sat with his back against the trunk. He fished his book out of his small backpack—he was rereading *The Lathe of Heaven*, by Ursula K. Le Guinn—and leafed through it until he found his spot, reading for a few pages.

Soon, however, he laid the book down and looked at Brutus, lying next to him with his massive head perched on his knee. "I think it's too nice a day even to read. There's only one thing for it. A nap."

Brutus agreed with him by already being asleep. Nathaniel leaned his head back, laid the book over his eyes and, thanks to the serenade of the stream and the birds overhead, was asleep instantly.

A WEEK LATER, JON DROPPED by before Nathaniel went to work at the hospital. It wasn't unusual for Jon to stop by unexpectedly, but it was out of the ordinary to do so when he should have been at work.

"Have you seen what's on YouTube?"

Nathaniel actually laughed a little, and then, so did Jon.

"Of course not. What was I thinking? I forgot I was talking to a Cro-Magnon man. One of these days, you've really got to get internet here in the house."

"I will," Nathaniel agreed, "as soon as you can give me a single valid reason as to how it will improve my life."

They'd had this conversation a number of times before, and Jon knew he held the losing cards, so he said, "Okay. Let's back up. You know what YouTube is, right?"

"A website where I can go if I want to listen to album cuts of John Coltrane or Chet Baker? Which, by the way, is the closest I've come yet to a valid reason why I might want to get the internet here. Close, so close."

"Yes, right. Musical clips. But, people can shoot their own videos and upload them, too."

"Lovely. Video democracy in action."

"Sometimes, not so lovely. Here, look at this." Jon took his smart phone out of his pocket, did a quick search, then turned the phone sideways. It showed a clip of someone walking through a wooded area, taking videos of various flora and fauna.

As he did, he gave a running commentary of what he was seeing, punctuated with, "Oh, isn't that a beautiful specimen," or "Would you look at that? What a gorgeous example of Polystichum munitum."

"I know, I know," Jon said. "Not exactly scintillating stuff, but keep watching." He tapped the screen and moved the slider bar at the bottom. The camera jumped and panned as the narrator nearly tripped over a root, but then steadied on an image: a pair of legs and hiking boots floating six inches off the ground.

"What in the world?" the narrator said. The cameraman moved the shot slowly up the torso, which also was floating above the ground. Just before he panned up to the head, a huge series of barks came from his left, and the camera dropped to the ground and showed only dirt and pine needles. Shortly after that, the video ended.

"Good thing he didn't get your face or Brutus on tape, or the jig would be up. But it's still not good, is it?"

Nathaniel shrugged, and said, "I'm still not sure why I do that. I don't really have any control over it." He tapped the video and scrolled down to read the comments. "Ha! Look at this. God love the internet."

Jon took his phone back and read. He shook his head. "I saw this same trick on America's Got Talent." "Fake news!" "Nice try, bozo, but people have been doing this trick in India for generations." He looked up at Nathaniel. "They don't believe it. They think it's a hoax."

"Of course they do. Why would they believe their own eyes, when they can believe their own sense of ironic detachment?"

"Should I report it, maybe get it taken down?" Jon asked.

"No, no, it's hilarious. If I had internet, I'd set it to stream constantly, to remind myself not to fall asleep in the woods."

Chapter Twenty-Two

Violet Moon was in her late fifties, and the firm lines of her chin had settled into softer edges. Woe be to anyone who thought her actually soft, though. Her laugh lines had deepened, and the years allowed her fear to lessen. As the years and decades had passed, she had done her best to forget about her life in Minnesota, and, to a lesser extent, Arkansas. For her, life had begun anew the night that she, Andi, and Nathaniel had rolled into Middle Falls.

She had been the director of the Middle Falls Medical Center for ten years, and had offers to run larger enterprises, if she had been willing to move north to Portland, or south to San Francisco, but she didn't consider it.

Just as Nathaniel had no interest in being promoted from swing shift custodian, Violet had no thoughts of ever leaving Middle Falls for career advancement. Five years earlier, she had bought an exceptional two-story house in a good neighborhood, with quiet neighbors, and she was completely settled into her life.

Violet had spent her early life bending to the will of others, just to survive. She had promised herself she would never be in that position again. She had made protecting Nathaniel her number one priority, but had to admit that he didn't need a lot of protecting any more. He was capable of handling any adversity that came his way, not to mention the fact that he had Jon and Brutus to protect him.

She hadn't been thrilled when Nathaniel told her that his life's ambition was to work sweeping and dusting Middle Falls Hospital.

"I know you could be so much more, have so much more," she had said.

"More what? More money?" he had answered. "I couldn't care less about money. More responsibility? To what end? Working my way up the corporate ladder? I'll keep my peace of mind and stay happily on the ground floor. I only want two things. To live a normal life, and to help as many people as I can, in my own way. I can do both those things as a janitor at the hospital."

They had never spoken about it again, and over the years, she had come to accept the wisdom of his decision and kept any further doubts to herself.

Violet and Nathaniel both worked Monday through Friday, so they made sure they got together every Saturday evening for dinner and a movie. They took turns picking the food and the film every other week. Many weekends, Jon and Melissa spent their Saturday nights overseeing slumber parties, but they were still able to get away from time to time.

This particular Saturday was one of those nights. Nathaniel's theme for the weekend was "Fish and Film." In that vein, he had chosen a spread from *Sushi Sushi*, and *The Incredible Mr. Limpet*, the classic film where Don Knotts got turned into a fish. Nathaniel and Jon loved the movie, but Violet and Melissa were less than thrilled.

"That's it," Violet said, "We're watching *The Notebook* again next week. But," she said, deftly plucking a California Roll and popping it into her mouth, "I have no complaints about the food."

Nathaniel scooped up Katie, put her on his hip, and stood facing Violet, Jon, and Melissa. "Ladies and gentlemen, I present to you, for one night only—"

"—we hope," Violet interjected.

"—hush, Mom. You can make me pay next week. For one night only, the wit, wisdom and absolute genius of Mr. Don Knotts." He pressed play on the remote and hunkered down on the floor with Kate on his lap. "Best movie ever," he whispered to Katie, who giggled happily.

A blare of trumpets, and the Warner Brothers Home Video logo appeared on the screen.

At that moment, the doorbell rang.

Jon jumped up and said, "I got it, I got it. Probably the paperboy wanting his two dollars." Without looking, Nathaniel reached up and gave Jon a fist bump for the *Better Off Dead* reference. "Don't stop it, I've seen this at least six times. I'll catch up."

Jon walked down the hall and opened the front door. A smallish man with long dishwater blond hair and a thin mustache stood on the porch. He held an old cap in his hands and smiled, almost apologetical-ly. "Hey," the man said in a strong Southern drawl. "Vivian here?"

Jon cocked his head. "I think you've got the wrong place. Hang on just a second, I don't actually live here." Over his shoulder, Jon raised his voice and said, "Violet, there's somebody here looking for some-body named Vivian. Anybody you know?"

In the living room, Violet shot a surprised glance at Nathaniel. A moment later, both Violet and Nathaniel appeared in the hallway and eyed the man outside.

Violet stepped toward the door. "Can I help you?"

The man smiled tentatively. "Vivian, is that you?"

Violet blanched, but did her best to smile. "Wh—who are you?"

"I shouldn't expect you to recognize me. It's been a long time—more than thirty years. It's me, Harry Spitton. You probably re-member me as Pup—that's what everybody always called me. I've come a long ways, looking for you and your boy."

Chapter Twenty-Three

"Pup?" The color drained away from Vivian's face. "Really?" She stepped forward and peered at him. "My God, you look exactly the same. I should have recognized you sooner."

"I'm sorry to just stop by without calling, but I didn't have a number for you."

"How in the world did you find us?" There was a hint of the old fear in her voice.

Pup nodded at Nathaniel. "Him. Your boy shines like a lighthouse in the dark to me."

Nathaniel stepped forward and reached out a hand, but Pup ignored it and wrapped him in a hug. Nathaniel laughed a little, then hugged him back, and held him out at arm's length. "Hello, Pup."

When Nathaniel had healed Pup, he had been four and Pup was in his mid-twenties. Now, more than thirty years later, Nathaniel was half a foot taller, and actually appeared to be a little older of the two.

It was an odd scene—Jon, Melissa, and Kate, all staring, unsure what to make of what was happening, while Vivian, Nathaniel, and Pup had a reunion of sorts.

"I don't understand," Violet said. "Shines like a lighthouse?"

"Huh. I figured you knew all about it. Not long after Nathaniel saved my life, I realized I could ..." He hesitated, looking for words to describe something he had never needed to explain. "Well, it was like I was connected to him. I could always kind of, I don't know, *feel* where he was."

Violet looked at Nathaniel. "Did you know that?"

Nathaniel shook his head. "No. It's got to be a one-way thing, or I would have felt you coming, Pup."

"Do you think that anyone you helped could do that?" Vivian asked.

"Oh, like Byron Creech?" Pup answered. "Yeah, for sure, for sure. Him and me talked about it once. Never talked to nobody else, though, 'cuz there weren't no reason to. We both felt it, though."

Nathaniel looked at his mother. *Fight or flight coming out in her again.*

Nathaniel put his arm around Violet. "Mom, it's okay."

"It doesn't feel okay to me, Nathaniel. I've been hiding from Cyrus Creech and his God Patrol for more than thirty years. Now I know he and his son have a direct pipeline to us?"

"It's not like that. Is it, Pup?"

Pup looked puzzled. "Oh! Are you afraid that Byron or I would tell Mr. Creech how to find you? We'd never do that."

"Look at it this way," Nathaniel said. "They've been able to lead someone to us all this time, and they never did. Why would they start now?"

Pup stepped toward Violet. "Your boy saved our lives. Why would we ever do anything to hurt him, or you? We never would—we're part of the same family now, in a weird way."

Violet took a deep, calming breath. "Okay. Not to be rude, then, but why are you here?"

Pup looked at the floor, slightly embarrassed. "Missus, take a closer look at me. How old do I look?"

"Mmmm. You still look young. Maybe 30 or so? But, I know you've got to be older than that."

"Right. I was 28 that day that Nathaniel saved my life. I'm sixty-three now, but I look pretty much the same as I did that day. Not that

I'm Mathew McConaughey or anything, but I don't seem to be getting any older."

"It was a shock to see you show up out of the blue like this, but now that I know who you are, you do look pretty much the same," Violet said.

"And you know, that gets to be a problem. I went to my class's 30th reunion, and that's where everyone noticed. Everyone else was older, a little paunchier, a lot less hair. You know, natural stuff. They took a picture of all of us and put it in the local paper, and that's when the whispering started around town. Mrs. Kelton, at the diner, asked if I had a picture in my attic getting old instead of me."

Pup looked at Jon and Melissa. "I'm from Tubal, Arkansas, which is a town so tiny, you can walk it end to end in less than five minutes and not be out of breath."

Jon nodded, but Nathaniel could see he was still not clear at all on what was going on.

"I tried dyeing my hair gray, but that just looked weird, and I ended up cutting most of it off myself. Finally, a few months ago, I decided the thing to do was just move on, find a job somewhere else, a long ways away from Tubal, where no one will know me."

"And you chose Middle Falls?" Violet asked.

Pup laughed at that. "No, I don't think I could live out here. It feels too different to me, and it's rained more in the last twenty-four hours than I usually see in six months. I like life to move a little slower. I think I'll try West Texas. Nobody there knows me, so I can kind of start over. But, before I did that, I wanted to drive out here and say thank you for my life."

He turned to Nathaniel. "You saved my life, and I didn't even know it at the time, but by the time I did, you was gone. So, thank you. I know Byron appreciates it, too. He's got the same problem, kind of—he kept getting older until he was grown, but then he stopped. He's forty-two now, and looks like he's about eighteen. He can't just pack up and leave, though, cuz he's second in command at his daddy's company, which is a heckuva lot bigger than it used to be. One word of warning, though. Last time I spoke to him, he said Cyrus was still trying to find you guys."

"Thanks for letting us know, but I'm not a little boy any more. We've got friends here, and nothing you've told me has me worried. There's really nothing to thank me for. I was so young, and I didn't really have any idea what I was doing. It's like I saw a puzzle in front of me, and I wanted to put it back together."

"Well, since that puzzle was my insides, I'm grateful you did. It's been a good life, and it looks like I've got a lot more of it coming. Gonna try to make the best of it. Oh, one other thing. Everyone in town always figgered that Andi Riley went with you when you left, cuz no one ever saw her again. Did she?"

A shadow of pain crossed Violet's face. "She did. She died in a car accident quite a few years back, now."

"Well, shit." He touched his hand to his mouth in surprise. "Sorry. And, sorry to hear that. She was a nice girl." Pup looked at everyone assembled around him in the entryway. "I've intruded on your night long enough. This is probably the closest I'll ever get to the Pacific, so I'm gonna drive over there and get my feet wet in it before I head for Texas." He slipped his Peterbilt cap back on and opened the door. He turned half way out, and said, "You've got nothin' to worry about from us, ever. We'd no more hurt the two of you than we would ourselves."

Pup nodded a good-bye and closed the door behind him.

Violet walked to the window and watched him climb into an older van still boasting Arkansas plates parked just down the block.

"I'm still worried, I would have thought you would have sensed him coming."

Nathaniel laughed. "I'm just a man, Mom, I don't have spidey-sense. But, I keep coming back to this—either Pup or Byron could have tracked us down any time they wanted to in the last thirty years, and I never would have seen them coming. Why would they change now?"

"You're right, I'm sure. Still, I don't like it. But, I think we're too wired into this community to just bug out again. And if they can see you wherever you go, it wouldn't matter if we did."

Chapter Twenty-Four

The following Monday evening, Nathaniel was back at Middle Falls Hospital, going about his rounds, but his mind was not as quiet as it normally was.

I can see some of what is ahead, but there are so many blind spots. Pup and Byron were in one of those blind spots. No idea what else might be waiting ahead. Something is drawing closer, though. I can feel it. I'm going to stand at a crossroads soon, and I don't know which way to go.

He knelt and, pulling a rag out of his back pocket, wiped a spot where something had spattered onto a door into one of the rooms. He looked up to see a woman lying in bed looking at him.

"Sorry to bother you. Just wanted to get that."

"It's no bother," the woman said in a small voice. "Nice to see someone other than doctors and nurses in here."

"Is that so? Well, I'll be taking my lunch in a couple of hours. Would you like it if I sat in here with you to eat it?"

The woman lifted her head off the pillow a few inches to get a better look at him, and Nathaniel could see the effort it cost her. She dropped her head back with a sigh and said, "Yes, that would be nice, if you don't mind. It could be your good deed for the day."

Nathaniel flashed her the Boy Scout salute, tapping three fingers against his forehead, and tipping her a wink. "It's a date."

He moved his cart around the corner to the family bathroom, took out his sanitizing spray, and continued on his routine.

A few minutes past eight, he slipped into the woman's room, thinking she may very well have gone to sleep by then, and not wanting to wake her. She was propped up on her pillow, though, wide awake and waiting for him.

"I'm Nathaniel," he said, sitting in the visitor's chair next to her and unrolling his lunch bag. He had made a salad with some of the last pickings from his garden.

"I'm Veronica McAllister. My friends call me Ronnie."

"What would you like *me* to call you?"

A phlegmy laugh and a small smile. "You can call me Ronnie. Thank you for asking. I don't mind informality, but I admit that I don't like it when it is assumed."

Nathaniel never asked the people he had lunch with, *What are you here for?* He knew that if patients wanted to talk about their illness, they would. Some patients couldn't be *stopped* from talking about what was wrong with them.

"Do you mind if I eat while we talk?"

"Of course not. What do you do here, Nathaniel?"

Around his first bite of arugula and butter lettuce, Nathaniel said, "I'm a custodian. That's why I was cleaning your door."

"Of course, of course," she said, already having forgotten the circumstances of their initial meeting several hours earlier. "Please excuse me. My memory is normally good, but," she said, pointing to the IV bag, "whatever they've got me on is throwing me for a loop. It's all right, I think I'd rather not be in my right mind at the moment."

Nathaniel took her in. Wispy white hair that was sticking up at all angles. Eyes that were fogged with opiates, but still filled with pain. He sat his salad down on her tray and scooted forward a few inches. He reached his hand out to her, palm up.

With no hesitation, she laid her own hand inside it.

She sighed, and then her eyes flew wide.

"Oh, my. What's that? What did you do?"

"Nothing much, and nothing permanent. I just thought it would be nice if the effects of both the pain and the narcotics were gone while we talked."

Veronica frowned. "You are not a normal custodian, are you?"

"I'm not really a normal anything. But then, who is? Normal is overrated."

She took a deep breath and gave a small whoop. "I haven't felt this good in so very long."

"Good. Do you want to tell me about your life?"

"Are you the Angel of Death, come to collect my soul?"

"I promise, no. I am really the Middle Falls Hospital custodian, come to collect your garbage, as soon as I eat my dinner. I would think the Angel of Death would be too busy to sit and eat with each soul he collected."

"Well, I'm afraid you're going to be disappointed in anything I have to tell you. I didn't really live my life. I let everyone else live it for me. First, my parents, especially my mother. Then, I got married right out of high school. Moved from my childhood bedroom into the house my husband already owned. No matter what I did, how many floral printed bedspreads or checked tablecloths I put out, that house never did feel like it was mine."

She sat up a bit, then leaned back on her elbows. "This is amazing. I feel twenty years younger. If I'd known I was going to feel like this, I wouldn't have scheduled my suicide for tomorrow. It's okay, though. Even if the pain is gone, I'm ready to go. I'm tired, and I'm tired of this life. I wasn't very good at it."

"Why is that?"

"I let people run over me. I never stood up for myself. The next thing I knew, my life was ruined, I got so sad I could barely leave my house, and now, here I am, just waiting to die."

"Waiting to die, or encouraging it along?"

"Oh, dying was inevitable, and soon. So, I invoked Oregon's assisted suicide law. That's quite an ordeal in itself, but I've jumped through all their hoops. Tomorrow, I'm heading off to whatever is next."

"You said you weren't very good at life. I've never heard anyone say that before. What do you mean?"

Veronica set her mouth in a grim line. "I mean, I just let people close to me take and take and take, and then, when I didn't have anything left to give, they tossed me out the window like yesterday's trash."

She glanced at Nathaniel to see if he was actually listening. When she saw that he was, she continued. "I met my husband when I was just sixteen. I was working after school at the local drive-in. I was a carhop, and pretty cute, if I do say so myself." She blushed at the thought. He was older than me, and he seemed so sophisticated. He came in to pick up his laundry, and he seemed so sophisticated. He was in his last year of college. He saw something in me, I guess, because he asked me out. We got married the summer after I graduated."

She looked up at the ceiling, lost in the memory.

"It's funny, isn't it, how the bad times often start out so good? I thought we were happy. I know I was, at least. We had two daughters, and life seemed good. As soon as the girls were born, he became very controlling. He told me how to do everything—what kind of diapers to use, when to stop breastfeeding, everything. Maybe I should say, *his mother* told me how to do everything. The words came out of his mouth, but I knew it was really her words I was hearing."

Tears formed and rolled down her cheeks. She wiped them away absently.

"By the time the girls were teenagers, I knew I'd lost the war. He controlled everything—the checkbook, the budget, what we did and when we did it, what we ate and how I cooked it—everything. Right after our youngest daughter graduated from high school, he told me we were selling the house and getting a divorce. He'd had a girlfriend for a few years by then. I knew about her, but I had pretended like I didn't."

She turned to look at Nathaniel.

"Do you know what the worst of it was?"

It could be so many things, but no.

"No. What was the worst of it?"

"The girls. I lost the girls too. And, I don't blame them. Oh, they still sent me a card on Mother's Day and my birthday, but it was all perfunctory. They never came for a visit, or wanted to go shopping. And why would they? I never showed them anything about how to be a strong woman. I suppose if they knew what was happening tomorrow, they would come, but it would just be out of a sense of obligation, and I don't want that. I suppose they'll read about it in the paper."

"Who is going to be here with you tomorrow, then?"

"No one, I suppose. I think I'm going to leave this world the way I lived in it—alone."

"Would you like me to come and sit with you tomorrow?"

A small smile brightened her face and chased away the raincloud that had covered her face. "Would you? The worst part of this was thinking about doing it all alone."

"I will, but there are other options to consider. I could take this all away from you. Not just the pain, but whatever's making you sick. You still have time to change whatever parts of your life you don't like. You could repair the bridges that have been lost with your daughters."

"Who *are* you?"

"Nathaniel. Just ... Nathaniel."

"Could you really do that?"

"Yes."

Veronica looked at him steadily. "I believe you could." She stared down at her hands. Her skin was so paper-thin that blue veins traced a pattern across them.

"No. I had strength, but I was too afraid to use it. Now, I have found my will, but my strength is gone."

Nathaniel nodded. "I'll see you here, tomorrow."

NATHANIEL SHOWED UP at Middle Falls Hospital two hours early the next day. He stopped at the nurse's station and visited with several friends while the attending physician was in meeting with Veronica. After a few minutes, the attending, Dr. Grant, poked his head out of the room and waved at Nathaniel to come in.

"This medication has to be self-administered," he said. He sat a pill bottle containing two pills on Veronica's table and took a step back.

"Afternoon, Ronnie. It's a momentous day."

"Nathaniel," Dr. Grant said, "she is feeling much better today, although her long-term prognosis is the same, of course. Would you speak to her about what she is doing?"

"I am here to listen to her, if she has anything to say, but I am not one to try and persuade someone, Doctor. I believe everyone should be allowed to make their own decisions, whether I agree with them or not."

Dr. Granted nodded curtly, but took a few steps back to give them some small measure of privacy. He was required to stay during the administration of the dose and the aftermath, but he did not like the duty.

"Nathaniel," Veronica said, and her voice was clear. "Thank you for being here to see me off. I've known you less than twenty-four hours, and it feels like you are the only friend I have. I don't know how I would do this without someone to talk to."

"I've always believed your friends know you instantly upon meeting you, while acquaintances will likely never know you."

Her IVs had been disconnected, so her hands were free. She caressed the pill bottle and said, "Come, bitter poison, come, unsavory guide!" She uncapped the bottle and without hesitation, put the pills in her mouth and washed them down with water. "I suppose that's the Shakespeare everyone steals at this moment, isn't it?" She smacked her lips and made a face. "Well, those taste awful. I should have asked for whiskey to take them with, but I've rarely tasted it, and I don't want to cough them back up. I'm not sure the doctor would give me more."

She put the back of her hand against her forehead, closed her eyes and fell back dramatically. After two seconds had passed, she opened one eye, looked at Nathaniel, winked, and said, "Still here? Very well then."

Dr. Grant frowned and didn't seem to appreciate that she was not approaching the moment with the proper gravity, but he didn't say anything.

"Doctor, how long now?"

"There is a narcotic included that will ease you off to sleep in the next fifteen or twenty minutes."

"Plenty of time for a woman with no last words of any import. Thank you, Dr. Grant."

She turned back to Nathaniel. "Any last minute advice for the departing soul, my wise, young friend?"

Nathaniel sat, scooted the chair close, and said, "Only this. Know that you are safe. You are loved. You are perfect. No harm will ever come to you."

"If anyone else in this life had ever said that to me, I would have thought 'bullshit!' and run away as quickly as possible. Somehow I believe you. And yet, and still, I am afraid." She reached her hand toward him. "Will you hold my hand?"

Nathaniel took her small hand in both of his.

"There. Thank you. You are a blessing on this world. I am ready now."

She laid back, closed her eyes, and relaxed.

Nathaniel closed his eyes as well, found her in the darkness and embraced her. "You are free, Ronnie. Free to go to whatever is next." She smiled and turned away from him. He stayed in the darkness a few moments while he watched her go.

When Nathaniel opened his eyes again, he said, "She's gone, Doctor Grant."

Dr. Grant looked at his watch and said, "Can't be. It's only been three minutes. She might be unconscious, but I will stay here until it's time to declare."

Nathaniel knew better, but he tried to never talk people out of their misconceptions. He stood, laid a hand on the doctor's shoulder, and said, "Thank you for letting me be here."

He clocked in an hour early and began his daily routine.

Chapter Twenty-Five

A month later, Nathaniel had a week's vacation from his job at the hospital. He didn't really want to take the vacation time, and he didn't have anywhere in particular he wanted to go, but twice a year, his supervisor insisted that he take a vacation.

So, he spent the time working on his music, reading, hiking, and spending time with the people he loved.

On the Wednesday of his enforced vacation, he was in his basement studio, laying down a keyboard track for his newest composition, when he heard footsteps overhead. Brutus raised his head and cocked one ear and let out a woof.

Jon West came clattering down the stairs. "Something is going on at the school. Can you come with me?" He looked panicked, an unusual state for him.

Nathaniel didn't bother asking what *something going on* meant. Katie would be at the school. "Shall we take Brutus?"

"No. Come on, I'll tell you what's happening on the way."

Nathaniel jumped up from the keyboard and he, Jon, and Brutus jogged up the stairs.

Once upstairs, Nathaniel said, "Brutus, stay."

Brutus's head dropped, but he laid down to wait patiently for Nathaniel's return.

Once they were in Jon's SUV and underway, Nathaniel said, "Okay, you're freaking out, so tell me what's going on."

"Melissa and I both got a text just a few minutes ago. It said that there was an incident at the school, and they were in a lockdown procedure. I was out in the country, looking at a new building site for one of our clients, and I had to drive right by your place on the way to the school, so I thought I'd pick you up. Melissa's going to meet us there."

"Okay. 'An incident.' That could be anything. Is the local radio station saying anything?"

"I hadn't thought to check." He switched on KMFR FM, but it was playing an old Kool and the Gang song. He turned it off. "We only heard from the school a few minutes ago, so they probably don't have anything yet. The text from the school asked parents to not come to the school but to wait for further updates via text." He glanced at Nathaniel.

"So here we go," Nathaniel said.

I'm not going to say, 'It'll be all right' or, 'I'm sure it's nothing.' There's no way to know, and you know it, brother.

"Into the breach," Jon said.

They drove the last few miles to the school in silence.

When they were still a few blocks away from the school, they ran into a traffic snarl.

"I guess when you tell a bunch of parents their kids are in danger, but to stay away and wait for news, we don't listen too well."

"There's parking in the city lot up ahead," Nathaniel said. "Let's pull in there and walk over."

"Good idea. I'll go crazy, sitting in a backup like this."

They swung into the parking lot and were followed by several other cars with the same idea. They parked quickly, jumped out, and double-timed it toward the school.

Middle Falls Elementary was a single-story brick building, laid out in a "U" shape, with a common area in the middle covered in grass with benches around it. It was an older school, constructed in the early sixties, and had been well-maintained.

When Jon and Nathaniel approached the common area, they saw that a large rental truck had jumped the curb and was sitting at an angle across the grass. The back of the truck was rolled up, but the only thing they could see inside was blue tarps, which covered an unknown mass. There was a man sitting on the back bumper. He had a small, black piece of plastic in his left hand and a bullhorn in his right. He wasn't doing anything but sitting on the bumper, but he looked nervous and twitchy.

When Jon saw the truck, he said, "Oh, hell no" and broke into a run. In this lifetime, he hadn't played for the Ducks or the Raiders, but he was still built like the middle linebacker he had been in his previous life. As he approached the common area, a local police officer held out a hand to stop him, but Jon ran right through him. Two other cops standing nearby joined in and were able to stop him before he got too close to the truck.

Nathaniel ran up, grabbed him by the bicep, and said, "Come on, we've got to be smart about this." He turned to the officers who were holding him back, and said, "I've got him. He's not going to go forward. Right, Jon?"

Jon gave a slight nod, but couldn't tear his eyes away from the truck, and the man sitting on the bumper.

The cop holding his left arm said, "You guys aren't helping us, you're making things worse. We've got to move you back. We're clearing this whole area. If that truck goes up, this will be a smoking hole in the ground. Come on, move. Now!"

Jon tensed again, ready to bolt, but Nathaniel put a strong arm around his neck and whispered into his ear, "Come on, Jon. Be smart. Look in the guy's hand. I would guess that's a dead man switch. If we do anything to him right now, the whole thing goes up. That won't help Katie at all. Let's move back, then we'll figure out what to do."

Even as he spoke, more police and fire trucks pulled up and began forming a barricade with their prowlers and trucks.

Jon and Nathaniel fell back several hundred yards to a spot where a few cops were setting up barricades. Nathaniel looked behind them and saw a Middle Falls city truck with more barricade fencing stacked on the back of it.

"Jon. Jon! Let's help these guys set the barricades up. The sooner they get a perimeter set, the soon we can figure out exactly what's going on here."

"I think it's pretty obvious what's going on here," Jon said, pointing in the direction of the truck. "There's some crazy bastard wanting to blow himself up and planning to take a school full of kids with him. A school that includes my daughter." Jon's own eyes had the sudden glint of insanity. "We've gotta do something."

"I know, and we will, but we've got to take it one step at a time. Come on, let's give them a hand."

The two of them approached the city worker who was standing on top of the truck, handing pieces of the barricade down to other workers who were carrying them and setting them up.

"We're here to help. What do you need?"

The city worker looked at them, saw the size of Jon, and said, "You bet. I'll set each piece here, then one of you hands it on to whoever comes to collect it. The other, carry pieces to whoever's installing the barrier.

They went to work. Nathaniel stood at the truck, receiving pieces of the fencing material, and Jon carried, because it burned a little of his nervous energy and gave him a chance to keep his eye on the truck.

That scene hadn't changed. The truck sat as an oasis of quiet amid the chaos around it.

When they were waiting for the next person to come to the truck, Nathaniel turned to the worker and said, "Have they tried evacuating the school?"

The worker shook his head. "No go. That guy sitting there said that if one person pops their head out of that building, he'll set the bomb off and take everyone with him."

"Has he said what he wants?"

"To talk to the governor. He said he's not budging until the governor gets here."

"That could take a while."

"If you ask me, the governor's not gonna want to come near this mess."

Probably right. If he puts in an appearance and the whole place goes up, that's not good for a political career. But, meanwhile, there are a few dozen teachers in there, trying to keep hundreds of kids calm.

An hour later, the barricade was complete, and the truck was completely surrounded, with several hundred yards of space between it and the thousands of worried parents and spectators who had lined up on the perimeter.

Jon had found Melissa, and they stood at the far left hand edge of the perimeter fence, never taking their eyes off the truck, or the windows of the school. Melissa had brought Jon his binoculars, and he kept them trained on the window of what they knew to be Kate's classroom, but there were no faces to be seen there.

Two hours after they had arrived, much had changed. With the barriers erected, no one was milling around the area of the potential blast radius. Reinforcements for the local police had arrived in the form of the Oregon State Patrol, and a police officer stood just inside the barrier every twenty to thirty feet, his or her back to the bomb, watching the crowd. News stations from Portland had arrived and were setting up their satellite trucks.

As with so many of these kind of events, the first images came from people uploading videos from their phones to Twitter, Facebook, Imgur, Instagram and half-a-dozen other social media sites. Across America, and around the world, millions of eyes were on the same thing: a panel truck with a small, nervous man sitting on the bumper watching the crowd carefully.

The final addition was a sleek black helicopter that hovered just at the edge of the blast area.

The man on the truck watched the chopper for a minute, then picked up his bullhorn and said, "You've got one minute to move that bird the hell away from me, or the whole place goes up."

It took less than thirty seconds for the helicopter to retreat and disappear over the horizon.

The man used the bullhorn to say, "Thank you," then sat it down on the back bumper. He reached behind him and retrieved what looked like a brown flask. With his left hand, he loosened the cap, took a deep swig, then replaced the cap and put it back behind him. His right hand held tight to the small plastic device.

Jon watched the man's every move through his binoculars. "Look at his damn hand. It's shaking like hell. My daughter's life depends on some maniac not dropping that switch, and it looks like he's got the DTs." He turned to Nathaniel. "Okay. I listened to you. We moved back. We built the barrier. We waited for someone else to do something, but no one is doing anything other than making him famous. So, what's your plan?"

Chapter Twenty-Six

This is it, then, the point I've been waiting for, and dreading. The moment of decision is upon me, and it's easy to see now. There really is no decision to make.

Nathaniel looked Jon in the eye. He smiled, but it was just a quick flash. "I'll take care of it, Jon, but I'll need some help from you."

"You know I'll do anything."

"Let's step back from the barrier a little." Jon, Melissa and Nathaniel turned and walked away, and their spots were immediately filled by people who had been standing behind them.

"Look," Nathaniel said, pointing to a spot a few yards away. "Their gaps aren't quite right. That officer has too much ground to cover, and he's standing right where there's a little room between the fencing. I need you to slip through there, and when he tries to stop you, run parallel to the barrier. Don't move toward the truck, and don't let him stop you. Run toward the cop that's down there, and make them tackle you, okay?"

Jon eyeballed the somewhat paunchy police officer closest to them. "Yeah, of course, no problem. But, what good does that do us?"

"You just do that, and I'll do the rest. I hope." Nathaniel glanced at the truck, then at the school. "Listen, Jon. If this doesn't go right, I'm sorry. I think I can handle this, but there is no way to be sure. I've done my best to see what's coming, and I don't think it's going to end well any other way. So, if I foul it all up, and I'm blown into a thousand tiny bits, tell Mom I love her, and I appreciate everything she did for me.

And, if that happens, will you take care of Brutus? He's going to live a long, long time."

Jon cocked his head. "Brother, I have no idea what you're thinking about, but you know I trust you with my whole being. Godspeed."

Jon and Nathaniel pushed forward toward the small gap in the barrier. Jon had to push a few people aside to get there, and cries of "Hey!" and "Knock it off" were thrown at their backs. A moment later, they were at the barricade, and Jon didn't hesitate. He turned sideways and slipped through. The officer took a step toward him, but Jon took off at a run. Instinctively, the cop chased after him.

Nathaniel took advantage of the gap to slip through the fence and walked toward the truck. All eyes were on the hubbub Jon had caused, so he was twenty yards past the barrier before anyone noticed him. Nathaniel wasn't running, but was walking at a steady clip.

"Hey, somebody stop that guy!" one of the cops wrestling with Jon shouted, but no one was near enough to easily intercept him. By the time the officer farther down the barrier noticed him, Nathaniel was already past the point of no return—the area all personnel had been ordered not to cross.

They gathered in his wake, and shouted to him, telling him to return immediately, but Nathaniel walked on, as though he were stone deaf.

He crossed the street in front of the school, and the man sitting on the back of the truck noticed him for the first time. He stood on the bumper, peering at the approaching figure.

Nathaniel didn't start to run, neither did he slow down. He walked as though he was right on time for an appointment he had made long ago.

The man on the truck hopped down, picked up the bullhorn, and said, "Hey! Asshole! You trying to get yourself and everyone else killed?"

Nathaniel lifted a hand in greeting, but continued forward. Behind him, every television camera, every cell phone, focused in on him.

Soon, Nathaniel was close enough to him that he could read the design on the man's t-shirt. It read *Sic semper tyrannis.*

The same thing John Wilkes Booth shouted after assassinating President Lincoln. I'm tempted to ask him if he's a big fan of assassinations, but I don't think I'd like the answer, so I'll play it straight. Too much at stake.

Nathaniel looked the man over. Smallish. A week's worth of stubble. Eyes twitching left and right.

Nervous. That makes sense. I need to find a way to talk to him. To reach him.

When Nathaniel was ten feet away, the man put the bullhorn down and spoke in a normal tone of voice. "Are you deaf, or just stupid?"

Nathaniel paused, stretched his back a little, and sat down on the grass, cross-legged.

The man's mouth fell open. "Oh my sweet jumpin' Jesus. You must have escaped from the looney bin. How did they let you slip through? Just my goddamned luck."

"Hey. I'm Nathaniel. I'm not here to bullshit you. I'm not here to get you to change your mind about anything, but while it's just the two of us talking, how about if we agree to not bullshit each other. Let's just be honest. I mean, I'm just one man, unarmed, and I mean you no harm. What do you say? What's your name?"

The man reached behind him, where he had kept the flask. "My name is your worst nightmare, you son of a bitch." He pulled out a revolver and pointed it at Nathaniel's chest.

Chapter Twenty-Seven

O n the rooftop of a building a block behind the barricade, a SWAT sniper chinned on his microphone. "This is Blue One. I've got the shot. Over."

"On which one?" the SWAT Commander on the other end wondered. Into his own microphone, he said, "Do not take the shot. I repeat, do not take the shot. We have confirmed he is holding a dead man's switch. Over."

"Or if it's not a dead man's switch, it looks enough like one to fool us," he said to the man standing beside him.

"Roger," Blue One answered, and continued to watch the action unfold through his scope.

Down on the field, Nathaniel opened his arms slightly, palms turned upward.

"You can absolutely shoot and kill me, if you want. That doesn't gain you much of anything, though, does it? It doesn't make you or your cause look any better."

"It would make it nice and quiet again, like it was before you got here."

Nathaniel laughed. "True!"

The man himself laughed a little. "Ah, shit, son. Why don't you get out of here, so I don't have to shoot you? I'd recommend you turn around right now and get back behind that fence line they've got set up along there. There's going to be some fireworks here real soon."

"I just can't do that. Too many innocent people inside that building, and one of them is my goddaughter, who I have sworn on my life to protect, no matter the cost. My guess is you want to make a big statement about something, and you're willing to die for it. That's why you drove the truck up here hours ago, and now you've waited this long so the media would have time to set up and make you famous."

"I take it back. You're not so stupid, after all."

Nathaniel nodded, then looked to the west. The sun had dipped below the horizon, and he watched the final faint glow of the day fade away. He thought briefly of his small house, the peace and quiet, the friendships he had enjoyed there. Finally, he stared straight up into the sudden twilight, looking for an answer he could not find.

"Too late to look for God, boy."

"Never too late for that." Nathaniel drew a deep breath. "Okay, then." Nathaniel stood up and dusted the grass off his jeans. "Nothing else for it, then." He took three strides toward the man on the truck, whose eyes grew wide. He scrambled up and stood on the bumper, then stepped up onto the bed of the truck, so he could look down on Nathaniel. He pointed the gun at Nathaniel's chest and pulled the trigger.

The bullet struck him just below the breastbone and staggered him back a few steps.

Nathaniel closed his eyes, and the hole healed itself.

"Holy shit, what kind of cyborg-mutant-alien shit is that?

Nathaniel took three more steps toward the man.

The man on the truck, realizing the gun was no good, dropped it behind him. "You're making me nervous, boy." He held out the switch in his right hand and shook it threateningly.

"It's not me making you nervous. You're nervous because you know you're lost, and still hoping to be found, but it's almost too late, at least for this life."

The man glared at Nathaniel. "Fuck you, smart guy."

He reached his right hand out toward Nathaniel and dropped the switch.

Chapter Twenty-Eight

For a frozen moment, all remained quiet.

So quiet, in fact, that Nathaniel heard the switch nestle into the soft green grass.

As it did, the dual-fuse igniter set off hundreds of pounds of Tovex Blastrite Gel, which in turn erupted a dozen barrels of ammonium nitrate and nitromethane.

Hell came to earth.

The blast eradicated the truck, and the man standing in it. They were both simply gone. The heat, the pure, destructive, power of the explosion, turned man, truck, and contents into minute bits of detritus.

Nathaniel stood, only a few feet away, head bowed, arms extended toward the blast.

He was not eradicated. He lifted his face into the force of the blast and accepted it, sought it out. He pulled everything, every bit of it, into himself. The heat, the energy, the hundreds of pounds of nails packed into the truck to inflict maximum damage, all poured into Nathaniel, but did not destroy him.

Moments after the blast erupted, it was gone. The truck, the man, everything, was simply gone. Where it had once been, a single man stood, unwavering.

Nathaniel once again lifted his face to the darkening sky and elevated his fists. When his hands were at their apex, he straightened his fingers out and a blast of pure, white light poured into the sky. It continued for what felt like an eternity. The thousands who had gathered could only watch, squinting and shielding their eyes from the brightness. The entire area had become brighter than noon on a clear summer day.

When the light faded away, twilight returned. Almost instantly, frogs and crickets began to sing.

Nathaniel turned and looked for Jon. *You can go get Katie now, brother. She's safe.*

Uniformed cops and men in dark suits ran toward him in a full sprint. Nathaniel stood and waited for them. A moment later, he was surrounded. The men were agitated, fighting over who was in charge, whether it was a federal or local crime scene, and, finally, whether it was a crime scene at all. These were men who were used to following a straight-line narrative through life, and everything they thought they knew had just gone up in a beam of light. They were also mindful that they had just seen a man—a single, unimpressive man—do what they all knew was impossible. If he could do that, what else was he capable of?

Through the argument, Nathaniel stood patiently. He had no idea what was coming, but he knew that life as he had known it was over.

Chapter Twenty-Nine

Finally, an older man in a black suit, white shirt, and red tie approached the group. He still had a full head of hair, but it was pure white. The men at the fringes of the small crowd moved aside to let him pass. The man approached Nathaniel, cocked his head at him with a squint, and said, "I'm Special Agent Tim Johnson, FBI, Portland field office."

Nathaniel nodded, but didn't speak.

"Can you tell me what just happened here? Because I saw it with my own eyes, and I still don't have any idea."

"Sure, I can tell you. I tried to talk to him, but it was no use. He was absolutely intent on blowing up the school, and doing as much damage as he could. Once I saw I couldn't stop him, I baited him into detonating the bomb. I was worried that he might shoot me before he did that, and if he did, I wouldn't have been able to absorb the blast."

"Absorb the blast."

"Yes. I sought out all the energy of the bomb, all the damage it was going to do, then pulled it inside myself. I converted it to energy and released it in a way that wouldn't harm anyone."

"The damndest thing is, that's exactly what I saw with my own eyes, but I still can't accept that. Until we get this straightened out, we're going to keep you with us as our guest." Johnson looked around at the uniformed officers. "I don't want to take him back to Portland right now. Mind if we use your station until I figure out what I'm going to do with him?"

A Middle Falls police officer stepped forward and said, "That'll be fine. I'll let the chief know to expect us."

Johnson looked at Nathaniel like he was a bug under a microscope. "We'd like you to accompany us, and one way or another, you're going to. You're not under arrest, but we are going to handcuff you for everyone's safety on the way to the station."

Behind Johnson, an officer murmured, "Like a pair of cuffs is gonna hold a guy who just did *that*."

Nathaniel shrugged, and put his hands behind his back. Another man in a dark suit stepped forward and put the cuffs on him.

The rest of the crowd was still being held behind the barricades, but Jon had managed to break through again and ran up to the crowd of law enforcement officers. "Nathaniel! What the hell are they doing to you? You just saved everyone! Now they're putting you in cuffs?"

Nathaniel smiled, shrugged, and said, "I guess I'm going downtown. Tell Mom I'm okay, there's nothing to worry about."

"I will. I'll get a lawyer and get him down there ASAP. Don't worry."

"Will someone get this guy out of here? What kind of crowd control do you have going on?"

Two police officers grabbed Jon by the arm, but couldn't move him.

"Nathaniel," Jon said, and tears glistened in his eyes. "I'm sorry you had to do this, but thank you. For Katie. I'll never forget it."

A third policeman joined the other two and managed to drag Jon away. Before he was out of earshot, Nathaniel yelled, "Grab Brutus for me, will you?"

Jon lifted an arm in acknowledgement.

A Chevy Tahoe with darkened windows pulled up where the rental truck had been just a few minutes earlier. There was no sign of an explosion where it had been, just the tire tracks. Two more men in suits jumped out of it and held the back door open.

Johnson touched Nathaniel on the shoulder lightly. "Here's our ride."

TWENTY MINUTES LATER, Nathaniel sat at a table in a small room inside the Middle Falls police station. It wasn't nearly as big or fancy as similar rooms he had seen in movies. There was no wall with a big mirror on it that he would know was really a two-way window. Just a small table, two chairs, and a cup of coffee in a plastic cup. They had removed the cuffs, so he was unencumbered. Nathaniel took a small sip of the coffee and winced.

Mental note: don't do that again.

Nathaniel was left cooling his heels for an unknown time.

Don't know if that is because they don't know what to do with me, or because they want to give me time to get nervous.

Nathaniel straightened his spine, closed his eyes, and meditated. He was in the same position an hour later when Johnson came in, also carrying a cup of coffee. He sat down opposite Nathaniel, who opened his eyes and looked at him calmly.

Johnson took a sip of coffee and winced. "Oh, my God."

Nathaniel grinned. "See, common ground already. I thought about warning you, but figured you wouldn't believe me until you tasted it."

Johnson looked down at the cup in his hand. "How do you even do that to coffee?" He shook his head and pushed the cup away. "Look, Moon, I'm going to be completely upfront with you. We have no idea what we're dealing with here. None of us have ever seen anything like what happened, and we don't have a playbook for that. I thought we had a playbook for everything."

He opened a file folder and looked at the scant few sheets of paper. He held them up. "Typically, I have a lot more to go on than this. I can't even find a birth certificate for you. First record I have that you exist was when you started school at Middle Falls Elementary in 1984. You're almost invisible beyond your school and work records. No social media accounts, no cell phone, no anything. It looks like you don't even have a debit card, let alone a credit card."

"I like to live a quiet life. It's just me and my dog, Brutus. When my friends want to talk to me, they come see me. It's a good life."

Johnson looked a little wistful for just a moment. He turned over another sheet of paper. "Absolutely no police record. Not even a speeding ticket."

"I don't speed."

"You don't speed," Johnson said, distractedly. "Right. What *do* you do?"

"I'm a janitor at the hospital, but I'm sure you know that. I have a recording studio in my basement and I make music there. Based on the reaction of everyone who has listened before you, you probably wouldn't like it. I hike with my dog. I read. I tend to my garden and try to grow as much of my own food as I can."

Johnson wiped a hand across his face, then twisted his head left, then right. "What I need to know is, how were you able to do what you did today. Human beings can't stand a few feet away from a blast like that and live to tell about it. I've watched the film of it more than a dozen times, and from four different angles. I still have no idea how you did it, and I don't know if I should arrest you, hug you, or nominate you for the Presidential Medal of Freedom."

"How did I do it? Does it matter? You saw it with your own eyes. A dozen cameras recorded it." He put a finger through the bullet hole in the middle of his shirt, then lifted the shirt to show nothing but smooth skin underneath.

Johnson closed the file folder, glared at Nathaniel.

"Son, it's about to not be my problem anymore, because every damn television network in the world is playing that tape over and over in heavy rotation. CNN brought in a magician to explain how the optical illusion worked. Fox News brought in the Right Reverend Billy Halsteen to explain that it was God's miracle. I have a hunch that this whole incident is about to get blown up above my pay grade. That's why I wanted to talk to you now, while I have the chance."

Johnson shook his head and grimaced. Without realizing it, he reached down and rubbed his lower back.

"Your back bother you?"

"You a doctor?"

"Definitely not. What's wrong?"

"Ah, I don't think they have any idea. I hurt it about five years back, climbing over a fence, apprehending a suspect who was a lot younger and a little faster than me. They've done two surgeries on it so far, but nothing has helped."

"How often does it bother you?"

"Every damned minute of every damned day."

"Listen. You asked me how I did what I did at the school. I can't explain it, I can show you, if you want. First, I've got to ask you a couple of questions."

"Asking questions is my job."

"Humor me, and I'll be able to show you some of the answers."

Johnson paused, then finally nodded and said, "I'm game."

"How's your life? If I told you that what I was about to do would make you live a lot longer, would that be a good thing or a bad thing?"

"Live longer?" Johnson mused on that, letting it roll around in his mind. "More time to be out on the boat, enjoying retirement? Yeah, that's not a bad thing."

"Are you married?"

"Just to the FBI."

"Okay. I can fix your back for you if you want."

"Call me a cynic, but sometimes I don't even believe what I see with my own eyes, because I've experienced enough to know I can be fooled."

"I understand. You might believe what you actually feel, though. Hold out your hand like we're going to shake."

Hesitantly, Johnson did. Nathaniel grasped it gently. He closed his eyes for only a few seconds, then released him.

Johnson jumped like he had been shocked. He pushed his chair back and jumped straight up. He stretched his back like he had just woken up from a long nap. Then he shook his head, dazed.

Nathaniel leaned back in his chair.

"I've been in chronic pain for five years. There's never a time that it's not hurting, at least a little, and usually a lot. Except, right now, it doesn't. I can't even remember what it feels like to not hurt." Johnson twisted at the waist, side to side, up and down. He bent over and touched his toes. "I'll be goddamned."

"Good."

"What did you do?"

"I fixed it."

"Can you do that for anything?"

Nathaniel shrugged his shoulders. "As far as I know."

"Cancer?"

"Yes."

"Holy shit, man." Johnson glanced up at the video camera in the corner of the room, red light steady, recording everything.

"If you can do that, you've got to share it with the world!"

"Do I?" Nathaniel ran his fingers around the top of the cup of terrible coffee in front of him. "I help who I can, in the ways I think I can do the most good. I have always known that if the world knew what I could do, any chance of just living my life would be gone. Maybe now you understand why I live a quiet life. I've never wanted to attract attention, because I knew what would happen. I knew I would end up in a room like this. I knew that someone or something, some person, some organization, or some government agency, would want to take me apart to see what made me tick." He glanced around at the industrial green walls and slightly wobbly table. "I always thought it would be a slightly nicer room than this, though."

Chapter Thirty

There was a knock on the only door that led into the interrogation room.

"Yes?" Johnson said, annoyance obvious in his voice.

A younger man, also dressed in the de facto FBI uniform—dark suit, white shirt, tie—poked his head in. "Sorry, sorry, but we've got something brewing out here. There's a man who says he is this man's attorney, and he says that if we don't let him in to talk to his client, he's going to hold a press conference out on the front steps of the courthouse, questioning why we are holding him. Oh, and there's about a hundred reporters out there, and more arriving every minute."

"Damn it. Any word from Washington, yet?"

"Just that we're in a holding pattern. Keep him here, try to keep a lid on it. I think they're flying someone out, but they won't be here for hours yet."

"I didn't hear anything in there about suspending an individual's rights for the good of the nation. Mr. Moon, you have an attorney wishing to speak to you. Do you wish to speak to him?"

"I think I would. Yes."

"Surely they've got a bigger conference room in this place than this?" Johnson said to the junior agent.

The younger agent poked his head back out and had a muffled conversation with someone Nathaniel couldn't see. "Yessir, they do."

"Have someone fetch his attorney there, and someone to show us where the conference room is."

Johnson stood, stretched, and said, "Probably not much more I can do for you than that."

"Understood. Thank you."

"I'm likely to lose control of what's going on here. Some heavy hitter from Washington will be showing up soon, and I'll be shuffled back up to Portland. In case I don't see you again, I appreciate what you just did for me. I am a new man."

NATHANIEL WAS LEFT alone in a much bigger conference room, sitting at a long table with nearly a dozen chairs around it.

Still no two way mirror, though. Maybe Middle Falls just isn't big enough to spring for that kind of budget.

A young Middle Falls officer opened the door and escorted in an older man carrying a briefcase. He was just a few pounds on the wrong side of the scale, but had an open, pleasant face and distinguished gray hair.

He walked to Nathaniel, set the briefcase on the table, and offered his hand. "Nathaniel?"

Nathaniel nodded and shook his hand.

Interesting vibe. Not an ordinary man. Same thing I felt when I first met Andi, and Jon. Which means—

"Pleased to meet you," the man said, interrupting Nathaniel's thoughts. "I'm Thomas Weaver. I'm an attorney here in town. Your friend Jon West called me at home this evening and asked me to come down and possibly represent you. He thought you might need the kind of help I can provide."

"I've seen your office downtown. Right across from the library, right?"

"Exactly." Weaver took a yellow pad out of the briefcase and asked, "Mind if I sit?"

"I appear to have dragged you away from hearth and home late on a Wednesday evening, so I think you're entitled to a chair."

"Before we begin, Jon asked me to tell you that he's picked up your dog. He also believes you saved his daughter's life. Now," Weaver said, settling in, "I'm going to ask you a few questions, but if you need to know something from me, stop me any time. To be clear—I don't represent you yet. I will make this first consultation pro bono, but I need to know if you would like me to represent you. If so, then anything you tell me in this room will be protected under attorney-client privilege."

"That doesn't matter, Mr. Weaver—"

"—Please, call me Thomas—"

"—sure, Thomas. In any case, privilege doesn't matter here. I've got nothing to hide. I did nothing wrong. I just did something unusual, and now, the government is involved. That's never good. But, at the same time, it would be good to have someone who understands the law advising me. So, yes, I would like to hire you to represent me. Do you require a retainer?"

"No, none needed. Let's see where this is headed first. Okay. Okay, okay," he said absently, putting pen to pad. "Have they told you if you are being charged with anything?"

"No. I'm not sure what they would charge me with. Hindering a domestic terrorist in the commission of a felony?"

"Yes. Right. I've seen the footage. I think most people in America have seen the footage by now. Remarkable. One concern is that they might paint this whole thing as a hoax, whether it was or not. An illusion, like when the magician made The Statue of Liberty disappear. Governments don't like things they can't explain. Or, control."

"Just for reference—I couldn't do that. Make Lady Liberty disappear, I mean. Look. I know this all has to seem pretty odd, coming into it cold."

"Don't worry. I've seen some odd things in my lifetime. I know there are things that have no easy or obvious explanation but are true, nonetheless. We'll proceed from there. So. They can hold you for twenty-four hours without charging you. Or, if the feds get involved, which is likely, up to fourteen days, if they invoke the Terrorism Act."

"Mr. Weaver, what you saw on the tape is exactly what happened. If, for the sake of argument, we can agree that's true, what would you advise me to do?"

"Well, we have options. We can cooperate fully. Essentially let them do with you what they will while they investigate. But I don't think that's the right choice. Not that I don't trust the government, but I grew up with Nixon as President. I watched the Watergate hearings for fun. I'm naturally suspicious."

Weaver jotted a few notes to himself on his legal pad.

"Another option would be to fight this through the normal chain of events. That's probably the safest path. In all likelihood, I can get you out of here within those twenty-four hours. They're going to have a hard time showing you as a terrorist."

"Are those my only options?"

"Well, no. This case is extraordinary. Nothing since 9/11 has gained so much attention, so rapidly. I could try to leverage that attention, that publicity, to get you released quicker. I don't mind a fight—it's what I get paid to do. But, it's a question of what gives us the best chance of success. The key question is, what do you want out of this?"

Nathaniel said, "Huh," to himself. "What I'd like is to be able to go home to my house, my dog, and my friends. Maybe have a beer with Jon and talk about this. I'd like to go back to work at the hospital next week, when my vacation is up. I'd like this to all blow over." He looked at his attorney. "But, I don't think that's likely, do you?"

"I had to park three blocks away, because everything closer was taken up by network news trucks and reporters. Your friend Jon said they're already parked up and down the road you live on, staking out your house. He had to fight his way through them to pick up your dog."

Weaver's smart phone chimed an alert. He thumbed it open, then read for a moment. "That's from my assistant. He says we're being swamped with interview requests, both for me, and for you. I don't see any way that this will blow over soon."

Chapter Thirty-One

There was a sharp rap on the door, then an Oregon State trooper, tall and intimidating, stuck his head in and motioned Thomas Weaver over. Thomas stood and walked quickly to him. They put their heads together in a whispered conference. Eventually Thomas nodded, and returned to the table.

"Well, that's interesting," Weaver said, pitching his voice low and confidential. "There's someone that wants to meet with you, and I think it will be beneficial to our cause."

"By all means," Nathaniel said, with a sweep of his hand and a smile. "I don't have any illusions that I'm running the show around here, anyway."

Nathaniel and Thomas sat looking at each other, Thomas drumming his fingers for a minute. Finally, Thomas said, "Hey, do you want me to see if they've got any coffee on?"

"God, no!" Nathaniel said, just as the door opened and Edward Buchan, the Governor of the great state of Oregon walked in, accompanied by the same State Trooper and a young man with an iPad and a worried expression. Governor Buchan looked the part of a twenty-first century governor. He was tanned—but not *too* tanned - with dark hair graying at the temples, and fashionable—but not *too* fashionable - glasses.

He strode across the room to Nathaniel, hand extended. Nathaniel, sitting with his legs crossed, was caught off-guard at the presence of the governor. He did his best to untangle himself and accept the governor's handshake.

"Mr. Moon, I recognize you from the extraordinary video I saw earlier, and the pictures they've been broadcasting ever since." Governor Buchan leaned forward slightly and peered deeply into Nathaniel's eyes—a long-held habit that had caused many a government employee to wilt. "Truly, extraordinary," he said, as if to himself. He gestured at the chair beside Nathaniel. "May I?"

It's tempting to say, 'It's your state, you can sit wherever you want,' but this is probably not the moment.

"Of course."

"I'll get right to it, then. Mr. Moon, you did a tremendous service for everyone today, but especially for me. I was in Eastern Oregon, doing an inspection of an area that had been ravaged by wildfires when this whole ordeal started. I did my best to get here to resolve this in a timely manner, but before I could, it seems you handled it on your own. And now, I owe you a particular debt of gratitude. You see, my granddaughter Marla attends that school. She's in Mrs. Adams' fourth grade class. If that madman had carried out his plans, she would almost certainly be dead tonight."

The governor shook his head, and Nathaniel saw tears in his eyes. *This guy's either an incredible actor, or a sincere and real human being. I'll go with the latter. But, what do you say to that?*

"I don't know how I could have gone on, if that had happened, and I know I share that with hundreds of other parents and grandparents. Now I've heard this nonsense about the whole thing being a setup and all that, but the people who would say that weren't there from the beginning, were they? They didn't face the impossible situation. You did. Oh, I'm sure that by morning, the crazies and uninformed will be spreading rumors and far-fetched conspiracy theories, but those are the fringe elements. Nothing to be done about them. They will always be there."

Buchan slapped his hand down on the table.

"Enough of that. I came here for two reasons. First, to tell you thank you. So from my wife and I, and our son and daughter-in-law, thank you from the bottom of our hearts for the incomparable gift you gave us. The second reason is, I want to know if there's anything I can do for you?"

Thomas Weaver raised his hand to Nathaniel, and spoke. "Governor, I'm Thomas Weaver. I'm Mr. Moon's attorney. At the moment, we're sitting in a police station, and we've been given every reason to believe that we're not allowed to leave. And yet, that is exactly what Mr. Moon would like to do. Is there anything you can do to help us with that?"

Buchan turned to the serious young man, whom he had not introduced. "David?"

"One minute, sir," David said, and hurried from the room.

Buchan returned his attention to Thomas. "The last I heard, the feds haven't passed on any instructions yet." He glanced at his watch. "Of course, that's because the whole incident is only a few hours old. I'm sure interference from Washington is coming. I'm just as sure they are scrambling trying to figure out what to do with you. However, until I hear differently, it's in the hands of the local authorities and the State of Oregon. Please know, anything I can do, I will."

The governor stood, shook hands with both Nathaniel and Thomas, and exited the room with the trooper in tow.

Thomas looked at Nathaniel and raised his eyebrows, as if to say, *Well, how about that?*

Minutes passed, and Nathaniel had come to believe he was destined to spend the night in the care of the FBI or the Middle Falls Police, when the door opened and Special Agent Johnson entered.

"You've got friends in high places, Mr. Moon."

"Only very recently. Until today, I was only a VIP at the Kwik-E-Mart, where I got every tenth cup of coffee free."

"You're moving up in the world then. The Governor has spoken to the Middle Falls Police Chief and me, and asked, as a favor to him, if we would facilitate your release sooner, rather than later. Since I don't have any reason to believe you actually did anything wrong, and since I haven't received any specific orders from Washington, I am going along with that."

"Great!" Nathaniel said, standing up quickly. "Let's go!"

"If I were you, I'd make some sort of an arrangement. There's something close to 200 reporters and cameramen waiting at the front of the station, and they'd all like a piece of you. If they see you leave here, you're going to have a lot of company tagging along. But, it's up to you. You're free to go."

Chapter Thirty-Two

Half an hour later, Thomas Weaver emerged from the front of the police station into the glare of klieg lights and camera flashes. He led a small entourage of people, including Jon West, Violet Moon, Ben Jenkins, another attorney in Thomas's office, and, in the middle, a tall thin man with a *Middle Falls High School* hoodie covering his head.

The group was bombarded with questions. "How did you do it, Nathaniel?" "Can you walk on water, too?" "Do another miracle for us!" That last wasn't a question, but it was heard repeatedly. No one in the group answered, but piled into Thomas's white Cadillac Escalade.

The Escalade pulled away quickly and drove off into the night in the direction of I-5. As Special Agent Johnson had predicted, a number of reporters piled into their own vehicles and gave chase. The rest of the group stayed behind and began to pack up their equipment.

After another forty-five minutes had passed, everyone except for a skeleton crew of reporters and camera people who were waiting for further instructions, had left. Initially, reporters had staked out the back door of the station as well, but when no one had emerged, it appeared they too had packed up and headed elsewhere.

Nathaniel Moon slipped out the back door and took a few steps toward a late model Toyota that had been left for him. He had only taken a few steps when he heard, "Hello, Nathaniel," from a voice deep in the shadows.

Nathaniel cocked his head in the direction of the voice, then peered into the darkness. "Jeff? Is that you?"

"In the flesh."

Jeff Hudson, a reporter for the local *Middle Falls Chronicle,* stepped forward. "Sorry, didn't mean to startle you."

"It's okay. You didn't. I knew someone had to be waiting out here. Glad it's you, instead of someone I don't know."

"Crazy day, huh?"

"You could say so."

"Have you always been able to do stuff like that? I mean, we went to school together, and I always knew you and Jon kind of hung by yourselves mostly, but ..."

"But, I didn't walk across the swimming pool, right?"

Jeff laughed, but said, "Yeah, exactly."

"I didn't wake up this morning knowing I could swallow a bomb, no. I didn't know I could do it until I had to do it. A lot of things in life are like that, right?"

"Sure. You hear about moms who lift a car off their kid, but I don't care how much stress I was under, if I stood that close to a bomb, they'd be picking up pieces of me in Eugene."

Nathaniel just nodded, but didn't answer.

"Don't suppose you want to sit down with me for an interview back at the office."

"You suppose correctly. What I'd like to do is be able to go home and see my dog and play some music, but I'm not sure that's in the cards for a while."

"They've definitely got your place staked out. If I was wanting a little privacy, I would head the other direction."

"Thanks, Jeff. Much appreciated." Nathaniel climbed into the car, turned the key and drove away.

As he did, Jeff Hudson used his phone to take a picture of the back of the car, with a clear shot of the license plates. He sent a text to a national reporter who had promised him five hundred dollars for good information, and attached the photo. The text read, *This is what he's really driving. Send the money to me at the address I gave you.*

NATHANIEL DROVE ALONG the back streets of Middle Falls, streets he had walked, bicycled and roller-skated for more than thirty years.

He pulled into the house of a friend of a friend of a friend, who was waiting for him on the front porch. When Nathaniel turned into the driveway, the man stepped off the porch. When Nathaniel emerged from the Toyota, he tossed him a new set of keys and nodded to a ten year old Ford Focus. It was blue, and was about as anonymous a vehicle as Nathaniel could have asked for.

"Thank you," Nathaniel said with a wave.

The man waved back and retreated inside his house.

The lengths a man has to go to in order to maintain a little privacy.

Thomas Weaver had orchestrated the whole escape for him—the person impersonating Nathaniel leaving the police station was Thomas's brother Zack, who was older, but had a similar build. It was also Thomas's idea to swap cars, certain that at least one person would see him leaving the station and record the license plates.

Nathaniel turned the key and slipped the Focus into Drive, then drove the streets of Middle Falls for ten minutes, back tracking, checking for a vehicle that might be following him, but he didn't see anything. Nathaniel reached into his jacket pocket, pulled the small phone Thomas had given him out and dropped it on the seat. Thomas had called it a *burner phone*. For the moment, it would be the only way anyone could get in touch with him.

He worked the back roads until he came to the entrance ramp to I-5 and got on heading south. The decoy group was almost an hour ahead of him, and they had pulled off at a prearranged truck stop just south of Albany. By the time Nathaniel arrived at the same truck stop, the earlier group had gone in, ordered and eaten, and departed, leaving one member behind—Violet Moon.

She was standing at the door, anxiously looking for him when Nathaniel drove in. She didn't wait for him to stop—she was out the door while he was still slowing down. She gestured to him to stay in the car, as she knew there were security cameras recording everything.

She jumped into the passenger side, and said, "Oh, Nathaniel, I am so sorry. Why do I feel like this is all my fault?"

"Because you like to take on guilt that isn't yours. Let's drive, and we can talk on the way. Where does the A-Team have me heading now?"

"Thomas said he didn't want to know where we were going. He was happy to play a part in getting you out of there. We're on our own again, just like we were all those years ago, when we left Tubal."

"Life is a series of circles, isn't it? Let's just drive for a while then, and enjoy our freedom."

Chapter Thirty-Three

Cyrus Creech laid in a twin bed in his cramped bedroom. A TV tray sat beside the bed, loaded with different pill bottles. He looked out his window onto a muddy, postage stamp backyard, and the back of his rear neighbor's house. A television played quietly at the foot of his bed. He was in his mid-seventies, but looked much older. Where he had once been thin, he was now emaciated. He had the look of a man with not many sunrises left in his lifetime.

Cyrus was no longer the wealthy man he had once been. Despite the best efforts he and Byron could put forth, Creech Co. had fallen into a familiar death spiral. Decreasing revenues had caused them to cut back on both raw manufacturing materials and personnel, which led to more decreasing revenues, and more cutbacks. After doing that dance for five years and with their noses barely above water, the Great Recession of 2008 finished them off.

Byron had gone to work for another company just so he could feed his family, and Cyrus had retired with his scant personal savings to a small home in a family neighborhood on the outskirts of Little Rock that he had once used as a rental. It was his only remaining asset, and he survived only by using a reverse mortgage to siphon his equity away, month by month.

Cyrus had long since given up any hope of finding Nathaniel. He had stubbornly held onto his investigative team and continued writing checks to them even through the first round of cutbacks at the company, but even he now had to admit he had held onto that chase too long.

Alice had left him a decade before, not because she was deserting the sinking financial ship, but because the older he got, the more dogmatic and pedantic he had become. Where once Cyrus had been a man of stalwart faith, it had continued to shrink and shrivel through the years until he had become bitter and judgmental. When Alice left him, she moved in with Byron, his wife, and their two children.

The topper on Cyrus Creech's misery cake came in early 2017, when he was diagnosed with pancreatic cancer. A quick Google search had revealed his likely fate, and in the ensuing months, he had resigned himself to it.

He was lying in bed, working on the project of thinking himself to death, when a strange scene on the television caught his eye. At first, he assumed it was a feed from the set of a movie, with the special effects already added in, because it showed a bomb exploding in the back of a truck while a man seemed to absorb the blast, then release it into the sky. The news program backed that portion of the tape up and played it, back and forth, several more times.

The next video the news program showed had a close up of the man's face. There are tremendous differences between the human face at age four and that same face at thirty-nine. Nonetheless, a name tumbled from Creech's cracked lips: Nathaniel. He knew it was him with the same certainty he knew he was dying.

He raised his head up off the pillow and clawed among the medicine bottles, looking for the television remote. He grabbed it and turned the volume up.

"I have a hunch this is all anyone in America's going to be talking about today," the newscaster said in voiceover. "That, of course, is Nathaniel Moon, who many are calling *The Middle Falls Messiah*. What exactly are we seeing here? Is it the kind of miraculous act that hasn't been seen since Biblical times, or is it all a giant hoax? Too soon to tell." The replay of the bombing disappeared and the newscaster himself was smiling reassuredly at the camera. "Whatever it is, you know we'll be right here to bring you the latest. Speaking of that, let's take a look at our five day forecast with Jenny Miller. Jenny?"

Creech switched the TV off and swung his skinny legs over the bed. He put his feet into his slippers and tottered toward the bathroom down the hall. Seeing Nathaniel, his great white whale, after so many years of searching had reinvigorated him. Yes, he was still dying, of course, but he felt more energy than he had in years.

Cyrus didn't have a cell phone anymore, so he got the house phone out and began making calls. Fifteen minutes later, he was pleased to know that he still had enough room on his one remaining credit card to book a one way ticket to Portland, Oregon, and to rent a car there.

He went out into his cramped, one car garage, filled not with his automobile, but with the remaining souvenirs of his once-successful life. Boxes of pictures of Creech posing with a string of governors and state senators. More boxes filled with awards – crystal shapes that read "Businessman of the year, 1992," and the like. Useless, most of it, but he knew what he wanted. He had been lying in bed envisioning exactly where it was that very morning.

Cyrus stepped around several piles and went directly to a black case that sat alone on a shelf. He retrieved it and returned to his bedroom. He sat on the bed with a wheeze. He was energized, yes, but he was still a very sick man who hadn't walked more than ten steps at a time in months.

He unlatched the box and removed the Walther P99 9mm semi-automatic pistol. It wasn't shiny black, but instead was a deep, dangerous green. He stroked the gun lovingly.

"I had one job for you, but now I've got something new. Let's see if the miracle maker can truly heal himself."

Chapter Thirty-Four

After an hour's drive, Nathaniel and Violet saw a billboard advertising "Clean and Cozy Rooms!" at the Standing Fir Inn, in Cottage Grove, just off the next exit.

"Been a long day, Mom. Let's pull off, and recharge a little."

They took the exit, turned right, and drove half a mile away from the freeway, before turning right down a tree-lined drive to a series of small cabins.

"I'd say if someone finds us here, they deserve an interview," Nathaniel said.

She went inside the darkened office and rang a bell that undoubtedly woke up the proprietor, who appeared a few moments later and sleepily checked her in. If he recognized her last name, he gave no sign of it. At 3:00 am, he might not have recognized his own mother.

Two minutes later, they were in the room, which, as advertised, was both clean and cozy. Cedar covered walls, the kind of generic paintings only found in inexpensive motels, and two relatively comfortable queen beds.

Violet sat on one bed and said, "I know you didn't have a choice. I don't know where we go from here, but I'm proud of you. If you had to reveal yourself, you chose the best way to do it. Our Katie is safe at home tonight, along with hundreds of other kids, because of you. If there's a price to be paid for that, whatever it is, it's worth it."

Nathaniel sat opposite Violet. He reached out and took her hands in his.

"From the time I was little—when I found out I could fix peo-ple—I knew this would come. I knew I would be faced with an impos-sible decision. When I was standing there today, and I looked into the eyes of that man, I knew it wasn't impossible at all, though. It was easy. I've spent too much of my life trying to hide this part of who I am. Now, I have no idea what's next, and that's okay, too. That's life, right?"

Violet nodded. "Let's get some rest, and we'll come up with a plan in the morning, because I don't have one now."

Nathaniel, who normally only slept two or three hours a night, laid down on the bed, closed his eyes, and didn't move for nearly eight hours.

THE NEXT MORNING, NATHANIEL awoke to find Violet al-ready up and out of the room. He took a shower, then was just facing the prospect of putting the same clothes back on, when Violet returned with two cups of coffee and a big shopping bag.

"Here. Coffee. We're on the run again, but we can still be human beings."

"It's got to be better than what they were pretending was coffee at the police station last night."

She smiled, then reached into the bag and threw Nathaniel a plastic bag with underwear, another with socks, a pair of jeans, and a powder blue t-shirt that read, in large, block letters, *COME AT ME, BRO.* "Here, you can change out of your towel. Sorry about the t-shirt. They didn't have much of a selection. It was either this, or one that said, *I'm with Stupid,* and I wasn't going to be seen with you in that."

"God forbid. Thanks, Mom. Hang on, and you can have the bath-room. I'm going to put on my nifty new clothes first."

Quick as a flash, he was back out, looking very un-Nathaniel like in his stiff new jeans and tight t-shirt.

"Oh, my," Violet said, almost able to stifle a giggle. "I believe I am fired from all future clothes shopping for you. And I used to do such a good job of it when you were a little boy."

"I used to rock those Transformers t-shirts."

Nathaniel retrieved his belt from his other jeans, then slipped the well-loved flannel shirt he'd had on the day before over the t-shirt and almost looked like himself again. While Violet was in the bathroom, he sat on the edge of the bed and turned the TV on. One of the network morning shows was on, and the first thing he saw was a video of the bomb blast.

Nathaniel leaned forward, interested in how it looked from an objective perspective. It was a wide angle shot of the scene. Across the bottom of the screen, a graphic was displayed—*Middle Falls Miracle*. The scene played out just as he had remembered it, but Nathaniel had to admit it was interesting to see it from above. The dropped detonator, the brief pause, then the incredible destructive energy of the blast. The network slowed the video down at that point, and Nathaniel saw the beginning of the destruction, before it all turned toward him, like steel shavings rushing toward a magnet.

In the video, Nathaniel watched himself stand completely still, gathering the force of it to him. *I thought maybe it staggered me, but no. Interesting.*

The focus of the video tightened, so that Nathaniel filled the frame. When he reached for the sky, the camera zoomed tighter yet. His face was alight as he released the energy.

The news show immediately began playing the clip again with expert commentary from someone who said they were a demolitions expert, but Nathaniel flipped away. The second and third channels were showing exactly the same thing.

Nathaniel switched again. It was a local station, and a pretty, middle-aged blonde woman was sitting across from an older woman. Nathaniel turned the sound up a bit. The blonde woman was obviously the interviewer, as she asked a series of thoughtful questions of the woman beside her.

"And what do you do with the funds you've raised?"

The older woman answered, "We are doing our best to diversify our efforts. So, in addition to buying books for youth groups and the like, we have also bought and refurbished an old bus that we can use as a bookmobile to serve areas that don't have easy access to a library."

Hmm. An interview segment dedicated to improving literacy among kids in a society filled with more screens than pages? Not your typical local news fare.

The blonde woman turned and looked directly into the camera. "That's all the time we have today. My thanks to Anna Hendricks for taking the time to come by the studio to talk about your literacy program. It's a worthy cause, and one I know our viewers will support. Thank you for tuning in, and be sure to stay tuned for the Thursday morning movie, *It's a Mad, Mad, Mad, Mad World*. Hope I got the proper number of 'Mads' in there. I hope we'll see you again tomorrow. I'm Laura Hall." The camera panned out on a low-tech set. A hand-painted sign over her left shoulder read, "Good Morning, Eugene." A scroll ran across the bottom of the screen that read, *Would you like to be a guest on Good Morning Eugene? Call us!* followed by a telephone number.

Nathaniel turned the TV off, just as Victoria came out of the bathroom, toweling her wet hair. She was also dressed in stiff new jeans. Nathaniel noted her t-shirt was plain, however.

"Okay. I think I've got our next move planned out," Nathaniel said. "I've got to make a few phone calls, then I'll buy you breakfast."

Victoria pointed at the small digital clock between the beds.

"Ah. Okay, I'll buy you lunch."

He picked the cell phone that Thomas had provided him, dialed the number he had seen on TV and waited. A woman answered, "KUET television, how may I direct your call?"

"Laura Hall, please."

A moment later, a young-sounding man answered, "This is Scott, can I help you?"

"Can I speak to Laura Hall, please?"

"This is Scott Neal. I'm Laura's producer. She's tied up right now. Is there something I can help you with?"

"Sure. My name is Nathaniel Moon. I was just watching an interview Laura did with a woman about her literacy program. At the end, there was a graphic that said if I wanted to be on your show, I should call, so here I am. I'd like to do an interview with Laura."

Chapter Thirty-Five

Nathaniel clicked the "End" icon on his phone and turned to Violet. "Well, there we go. At first, he told me that it would take them three months to get me on the interview calendar, but then I heard someone whispering to him, and now we're on for this afternoon. They said they couldn't afford to pay me anything for the interview. Do people usually charge reporters to talk to them?"

"When they're the most sought-after interview in the world, yes, they do. Are you sure this is the right thing to do?"

"I'm not sure about much, right at the moment," Nathaniel said as he thumbed the television back on. As he ran through the channels, he was the topic of conversation on more than half of them. "But I think the horse is out of the barn on keeping a lid on this, Mom." He reached out and put an arm around her shoulder. "I know that humans don't like change, but it's the one inevitable thing in our lives. We need to learn to embrace it."

"I can handle change, like when the coffee shops stop serving Pumpkin Spice lattes. I don't like it so much when our whole life get tossed in a blender and someone hits 'puree.'"

"It's going to be fine. I want to do this interview. I've got a few things I'd like to say, while I have the chance." He glanced down at his shirt. "Maybe we can try to find a different store on the way, though?"

THE KUET STUDIOS WERE a modest affair, a smallish building in the middle of an industrial area. A sign in front read, "KUET, *We Bring Life to Eugene!*" Violet looked at the building and said, "My one chance to meet Anderson Cooper, and you choose this little place. C'mon, let's go in."

Inside the lobby, there was only one young man there to greet them. He looked to be in his early twenties and was tall and thin with an excess of nervous energy. "Mr. Moon? I'm Scott Neal. We spoke on the phone. It's an honor to have you here."

"Is this place always so quiet?" Nathaniel asked, looking around at the empty and darkened offices.

"No, but Mr. Wagner, that's the Station Manager, wanted it to be as quiet in here as possible when you arrived. He said nothing this big has ever happened to this station. Not even when we had a cameraman up by Mount St. Helens when she blew."

"That's very kind. Where are we going to do the interview?"

"In our studio. Laura's in there waiting for us. She's been prepping all afternoon. I know she's anxious to meet you. We're lucky to have her here. She had her own talk show up in Seattle, but once her daughter was born, she wanted to find a smaller town to raise her in and she settled here. Seattle's loss is definitely Eugene's gain." Scott led them through the building and through a door that opened into the same set that Nathaniel had seen that morning.

Laura Hall was sitting in one of the brown swivel chairs and jotting some notes into a notebook, but looked up when the door opened.

"Mr. Moon, please, come in. I'm Laura Hall. I'm so pleased you're here."

"I saw your interview with Mrs. Hendricks this morning about her literacy program. I thought it was very well done." Nathaniel fished his wallet out of his back pocket and plucked out two twenties and a ten. "Would you be able to pass this on to her? I'd like to support what she is doing."

Laura looked a little flustered, but accepted the bills and turned to Scott. "Will you see that Mrs. Hendricks gets this? Please, sit down," she said, indicating the other swivel chair, "and let's go over the ground rules."

"Great. What are the ground rules?"

Laura laughed. "No, I assumed you would have some ground rules for me. Subjects or topics that are off-limits, areas that are sensitive for you, that sort of thing."

"Oh, sorry. I've never done anything like this before. I assumed you would be the one to tell me what to do. No, no ground rules for me. I'm open to discussing anything you'd like. This is the only interview I'm going to give, though, so the weight of the world is on your shoulders." Nathaniel smiled as he spoke this last, but knew it was the truth.

"That's very refreshing. I interviewed a Eugene City Council member a few weeks ago, and he sent me a six page memo of things that couldn't be discussed."

"This is the advantage of living a quiet life, with no political ambitions. I have nothing to hide, and don't need anyone's vote. How long do you think this interview will run?"

"I don't have a set time for it. I don't like to work off a specific set of questions. I prefer to just have a conversation and see how it progresses. We'll film the whole interview, but we might edit it for time before we air it. You have my word that we won't edit it to make it appear that you are saying something you aren't. We *will* use short slices of it in promo spots. If you feel like we've gone on too long, just let me know and we can wrap it up."

"Other than the open road, we've got nowhere to go other than here, so use me as you will."

"I have a makeup person standing by. Would you like her to make you up before the interview?"

"Oh my God, no. I can't imagine it. I'll be fine. By the way, is this going to be live?"

"No, no. We'll record it now, then we'll edit it together with some of the other footage, and we'll broadcast it as a special tonight."

"Perfect. That will give us a chance to put a few miles under our wheels by the time it airs. We have people who want to keep us company, wherever we go. I've been hoping that if I take the time to sit down and answer all the questions you might have, then maybe some of the interest will settle down."

"I'd like to tell you I agree, but I don't think so. I've never seen as much interest in anything as there is in you." She turned away from Nathaniel and said, "Scott, would you get us some water? If we run long, we might need it. Tell Larry we're ready, will you?" She turned back to Nathaniel and Violet. "I hadn't thought, would you like to be part of the interview, Mrs. Moon?"

"No, absolutely not. I'd enjoy watching it, though, if I could."

"Of course. Scott will be in the production room, if you'd like to watch it there with him."

Scott returned with a pitcher of water and two glasses, then escorted Violet back out through the door to the control room.

A bored looking man sauntered in and stepped behind the camera. A moment later, he peeked around at Laura and gave her a thumbs up.

Laura looked straight into the camera and said, "Nathaniel Moon interview in 3, 2, 1."

Chapter Thirty-Six

"Hello, I'm Laura Hall, and I am pleased to have the opportunity to interview Nathaniel Moon. If you've been anywhere near a television or any kind of screen in the last twenty-four hours, you have almost certainly seen the video of Mr. Moon's heroic actions in Middle Falls, Oregon. I've been in the news business for twenty-five years, and I think it's the most extraordinary thing I've ever seen."

She turned to look at Nathaniel. "Thank you for joining us. We are a small-market, local station. Meanwhile, every broadcaster in the world, from CNN to Fox News to MSNBC and the BBC is trying to have a sit-down with you, so I think the first thing I have to ask you is, 'Why us?'"

"I saw your show this morning, and I liked it. I'm not much for appearances. Celebrity doesn't have any currency to me. It's all transitory. Think of someone who was famous twenty-five years ago. Are they still sought-after today? Likely not. Two days ago, anyone in the world that wanted to, could have stopped by my house for a visit. I would have welcomed them, put the coffee pot on, and we could have talked about all the things you and I are going to talk about now. But I wasn't famous then. I am, apparently, today. But I'm the same person."

"Maybe that's not fair, though. Yes, you were the same person, but, to all appearances you were an ordinary man. You worked in a hospital, you lived alone—"

"—Except for my dog."

"—yes, except for your dog. So people may not have known you were capable of such extraordinary feats."

"Is that the standard, then? 'Can someone perform what the world will see as miracles?' If so, that's a pretty difficult standard to reach."

Laura, shifted, tapped her pen against her cheek.

"Let's change tacks a bit then. Have you always been able to perform 'miracles,' as you say?"

"Yes. But, I'm not alone. We all can. You could. Larry over there, behind the camera, he could."

Larry, who had been a disinterested observer, peeked around the camera with a "Who, me?" expression.

Nathaniel winked at him, then turned his attention back to Laura.

"Let's table that for the moment, and come back to it. You say you've always been able to do these things. Tell me about the first time you did something extraordinary."

"My first memory is waking up in my mother's womb."

Laura did her best to remain a disinterested third party, but her jaw fell open slightly.

"I know that seems extraordinary, but I believe we all do that, then we proceed to forget about it. If not by birth, then not long after. In my case, though, my mother was under extreme stress at the time, and we began to communicate."

"Wait," Laura said, raising her hand. "I just want to clarify. You're saying you were completely conscious in the womb—aware of your surroundings—and that you communicated with your mother."

"Yes."

Laura shook her head. "I can't imagine if my child had reached out to me in the womb. Frankly, I think it would have freaked me out."

"Now imagine that you are all alone, fleeing for your life from an abuser, and that happens. My mother is an extraordinary woman." Nathaniel glanced at his mother through the glass and smiled. Tears glistened in Violet's eyes as she fluttered her fingers at him.

"Did you perform any miracles as a child?"

Nathaniel paused, thinking. "When I was very young, I healed two people. My mom was, rightfully, concerned that things were going to spin out of control—basically, that she was going to lose me to a process she couldn't have stopped."

"I understand that. If my child performed miraculous acts, that's one thing. If I'm afraid that someone might take my child away from me because of it, that's something else altogether. So, bearing that in mind, how did your mother react?"

"We ran. We packed what we could into our car, and we left. We drove until we just about ran out of road to drive on, and that's how we ended up in Middle Falls."

"But you were still very young then, correct?"

"Yes. I was four."

"Four. But you've lived in Middle Falls ever since, correct?"

Nathaniel nodded.

"So nothing to attract attention to yourself? No more miracles, so to speak?"

"Not exactly. I still did my best to help people where I could. I just tried to do it in such a way that we wouldn't have to move again. I might have seen a neighbor of ours suffering from arthritis at the grocery store. If I just touched her arm when we said hello, her pain would go away. I did my best to be discrete. I liked Middle Falls. I didn't want to have to leave it. Plus, simple acts of kindness can add up just as much as a public miracle. If you see someone who is hungry, you can feed them. If someone is lonely, you can spend time with them. If you open your eyes, there are opportunities everywhere."

"All these years, then, you've essentially kept these miraculous abilities under wraps. Until yesterday, when you made quite a splash. What changed?"

"Perspective is everything. There are tragedies every day. More than eight million people die from cancer every year. That means twenty-two thousand families are having a very bad day, every single day. If I was able to save a new person every five seconds, twenty-four hours a day, I couldn't save them all. And, even if I could, I wouldn't want to."

"That surprises me. Why not?"

"We all have a hand in planning out what our lives are going to be like, based on what we feel we need to learn in this life. For example, if I feel I need to learn humility, I might choose a life that humbles me."

"You're saying then, that before we are born, we choose what kind of life we're going to live."

"We all have free will, but I think we each put a lot of planning into what the circumstances of our lives will be before we are born. Some lives can be like a vacation. We've all known people who seem to be good at everything, right? Pick up a tennis racket, and they're quickly beating experienced players. Sit down at a piano and just begin plunking out a song. Those lives are fun, and can recharge our batteries, but they're not good for learning anything. Success is a terrible teacher. We learn when we fail at something."

Laura opened her mouth to ask a follow up question, but Nathaniel continued.

"If I begin making wholesale changes in people's lives, including when and how they die, I will negate a lot of that planning. The divine part of me, which we all have, is able to think that way, to distance myself. But yesterday, my friends were in such pain, such fear that they were going to lose their daughter, that I interfered."

"According to what you just said, though, you would theoretically be harming them in the long run."

"I agree. That's why I don't think what I did yesterday was necessarily a good thing. It was likely a weakness on my part, or a test that I failed. That's the human part of me. I never said I was perfect. I just brought a little more perspective with me from my last life."

"Let's talk about the reactions to what happened in Middle Falls yesterday. As I was preparing for this interview, I read stories about you from around the globe. Let me read you some of the headlines, and, if I could, get your reaction to them."

"Sure."

"The Great Middle Falls Bomb Hoax."

"I wish more people believed that. It would make my life easier."

"Middle Falls Messiah."

"Not even close. What's the definition of a messiah? A person who wants to lead a group of people, or a cause. I have no interest in any of that. I don't believe such things, overall, are beneficial."

"Messiahs, or causes?"

"Both."

"Let's stay there for a moment. Are you saying that religion is bad? Christianity?"

"I don't like to label things like that. Here's the thing about humans: we fear death. We are afraid it is the long blackness, a total loss of our unique consciousness. So, we create stories, myths, of what happens to us on the other side of that curtain. That makes us feel better. It lets us ignore that fear of death for long stretches. But, there are certain things that are simply beyond our comprehension. In our human forms, it is almost impossible to truly comprehend the divine. But, that doesn't stop us from trying to quantify it, name it, limit it by using words to capture it. The divine is so vast, it cannot be reduced down enough for us to grasp in this form, but that doesn't stop us from trying. If I have a secret, it is knowing that the divine is inevitable. We are moving toward it at exactly the speed we are intended. No matter what we do, whether we expend incredible energy, or none at all, we will arrive there at the same moment."

Nathaniel paused, made eye contact with Violet in the control room. "I'm no theologian, but I see dangers in all organized religion."

On the other side of the glass, Violet hung her head and whispered, "Oh, Nathaniel, you know what that will do."

"Such as?"

"Dogma can act as a salve for the itch of self-discovery. If all the answers are bundled into a book, or a single philosophy, or act, that doesn't encourage you to continue to quest to find any other truths. When someone hands me a package, and says, 'This is all you need,' I am suspicious. And of course, there is the weight of history. If you take all the good that religions do and put it on one side of a scale, and all the harm it has done on the right, which weighs most heavily?"

"That's not likely to be a popular opinion."

"Good thing I'm not running for office. Have you ever looked at it this way? Why were all the miraculous deeds limited to ancient times? If men and women of God were able to manifest miracles then, why not now?"

"I'm guessing you have an answer to that."

"I have a theory. If say, Jesus Christ was on Earth now, and he performed the miracle of the loaves and fishes, what would result? He would be besieged with requests to end world hunger, to magnify his miracle a million fold. If he healed the lepers, he would be overwhelmed with crowds of the sick and dying everywhere he went, until he was stifled by them. His voice wouldn't be heard above the din of the crowd. In all likelihood, some government somewhere would step in and try to harness his miraculous gifts for their own ends."

"Does that same thinking apply to you?"

"Of course. If I could have walked and talked to people and helped those I could while sharing any messages I might have, that would have been a life worth living. In our world, though, we have vaccinated ourselves from miracles and miracle workers by creating a communication network that makes it impossible to spend the needed time with people. I don't think that if I spread my message on a Facebook page, or Twitter account, that it would have had the same impact. Even if I had climbed to a mountain top, I believe the lines would have stretched to the bottom. Do you doubt it?"

Laura shook her head, agreeing with Nathaniel. "You said just now that you had messages you would have been interested in sharing with the world. I'm sure this interview will be seen by untold millions for many years to come, so what message would you like to share with us?"

"One of my core beliefs is to not give unsolicited advice. But since you asked, I will tell you some of the things I believe. If you'll keep in mind that I am just as human as everyone else, and that everything I say might be wrong."

"All right ..."

"We look for happiness outside of ourselves—cars, television, houses, social media—but freedom and happiness can only be found within ourselves. And I don't mean to say this is a new human condition. Before technology became what so many worshipped, we had the same problem. People thought *If only I made ten thousand more dollars per year, I would be happy.* Or, *If only she would love me, then my life would be perfect.* Or, *If only God would bless us with a child, our life would be complete.* Here's an enduring truth: If you're not happy with what you have, you will never be happy with anything you get."

"Profound."

"I think I read that in a greeting card. You've got to find your life's truths where you can."

Chapter Thirty-Seven

Laura paused for three beats, then glanced at Scott in the control room. "Let's take a quick break here."

Larry stepped out from behind the camera and walked over to the set. He was a large man with a Rasputin beard that reached his chest. "Laura, I'm sorry, and I know we talked about this, but I'll never get another chance like this." He turned to Nathaniel, a pleading look in his eyes. "I have a little girl that's never walked. If she was here, could you make it so she could?"

"Would you want me to?"

"Of course!"

"Most importantly, would *she* want me to? She chose this life, chose her limitations, because she wanted to learn something. If I change that, she might have to live another entire lifetime. Would that be worth it to her?"

He looked nervously at Laura. "Would you ask her yourself?"

"Larry!" Laura said. "We all agreed that we would be professionals about this."

"I know, I know, but what if it was your little girl, Laura? Wouldn't you do anything for her?"

That hit Laura where she lived. She had given up her career and moved to a small town to give her daughter a better life. "Of course I would," she said softly. "Is she here?"

Larry didn't dare speak, but he nodded. Laura looked at Nathaniel.

"It's fine with me, but I don't want the camera on. It's not fair for her."

Larry said, "Thank you!" and hurried through the studio door, only to return seconds later pushing a young girl in a wheelchair. A woman, who Nathaniel assumed was her mother, trailed behind.

Nathaniel stepped off the set, walked to the girl and knelt in front of her chair so their eyes were at the same level. "What's your name?"

"Grace."

"Of course. Grace." Nathaniel looked deeply into her eyes. "And you are full of grace, aren't you?" He reached out and held her small hand in both of his. "Do you know what your Mom and Dad are asking? They want me to help you walk. I understand how attractive that is, but think, just for a moment. There might be reasons why your beautiful spirit chose this body. Maybe you are intended to inspire, to lead, but do it from this wheelchair."

Grace considered that carefully. "If I chose to be this way, I've changed my mind. I want to run with my friends. I want to go hiking with Daddy and Tuffy, our dog. I want that more than anything."

Nathaniel nodded, then released her hands and reached out to hug her. Grace laid her head against his shoulder. Nathaniel stood and smiled at her. "You can walk, Grace."

Effortlessly, she stood. Nathaniel opened his arms and she took two tentative steps toward him, then fell into another hug. She turned to her parents with a smile as wide as Texas.

"Goodness," Grace's mother said, crossing herself, then put her hand to her mouth as her tears flowed.

Larry looked at Nathaniel and shook his head. His eyes were dry, but wide with what he had just witnessed. "I have no words for what this means to us."

"I'm glad I came here, so I could help." Nathaniel shook hands with Larry and his wife, then stood in front of Grace, who twirled once, just to show she could. "You're going to have a good long life now, Grace. I hope you fill it with happiness." He turned and stepped back up on the set. "Okay, ready to go, Laura?"

"Y-yes. Mr. Moon, that was unbelievable. I've known Grace for years, and I've never seen her out of that chair. I cannot imagine the incredible responsibility you have."

Larry, his wife, and Grace all engaged in a long group hug until Larry broke away. "Hon, I've got to go back to work. I'll be home soon. Let's go out for pizza tonight to celebrate."

Grace said, "Yay!" and she and her mother left the studio, Grace pushing the wheelchair.

Laura did her best to recover her cool. She poured two glasses of water from the pitcher and handed one to Nathaniel. "These studio lights are hot."

"I was born in Arkansas. Heat has never bothered me. But, thank you," he said, as he accepted the water and took a drink.

"You look at the world differently than anyone I've ever met. I am so pleased you called us. When I woke up this morning, I thought the highlight of my day would be watching *Criminal Minds* reruns with my daughter."

"How old is she?"

"Thirteen. That horrible, arid desert between childhood and adulthood, when she's sure Mom knows nothing about anything. Do you have children? I've tried to keep the most personal questions out of the interview because I don't think they're relevant."

"No, no kids, no wife. I knew this day was coming, and I didn't want to expose them to this craziness."

"Understood." Laura glanced into the control room. "Larry? Scott? I think we're ready." She gave them a moment to get back into position. "I'll give us a countdown. In 3, 2, 1."

Laura's demeanor changed, from quiet and intimate, back to professional. "This is Laura Hall, once again with the man some are calling *The Middle Falls Messiah*, Nathaniel Moon. We were just talking about any messages you might have for the world at large. Is there anything else you would like to say?"

"Of course. There's always more to say. That's why rabbis have gathered in Temple for thousands of years. It's part of why coffee houses and bars are so popular. Well, aside from the coffee and booze. It's the communion. The *figuring out.* Some things we can only learn alone, but others, we learn by communicating with each other." Nathaniel paused, thinking. "Are you aware of *The Secret?* About the law of attraction, and how it works?"

"Of course," Laura said with a smile. "If it was ever on Oprah, I saw it. What do you think about it?"

"I think The Law of Attraction works perfectly, one hundred percent of the time."

Laura sat back. "Really? I'm surprised to hear you say that. I've known people who did their best to manifest things through visualization, and have had no success. If it works every time, why isn't everyone rich, thin, and happy?"

Nathaniel nodded. "Right. You're talking about conscious state manifesting. That's very hit or miss. Far more miss than hit, I would say. I maintain that each of us gets exactly what we truly want, on a deep, spiritual level. If people aren't rich, or thin, or happy, it's because that's not the path they chose to walk for this life. The life pattern that we set in motion before birth is much more powerful than what we think we want now. The system is wired so we can't change our minds midstream, essentially."

Nathaniel looked directly into the camera lens. Through it, almost, until Larry peeked his head around again and made eye contact with him. Nathaniel let a small grin play across his face, then said, "There are exceptions, of course, as there are to anything."

Larry nodded at him, smiling himself, tears now in his eyes.

Quietly, almost to himself, Nathaniel said, "And that's just as true for me, as it is for anyone. This is the path I chose for myself, long ago.

This is my lesson to learn. We choose what problems we want to have in this life, based on what lessons we think we need to learn." He chuckled a little. "Laura, I just had a breakthrough here, right before your eyes."

"The Master has a moment."

"If you will, yes." Nathaniel looked up into the bright lights, but in reality, he was looking beyond."

"It's nice to see someone like you is still learning, too. It gives the rest of us hope, I suppose."

"Oh, I still have so much to learn. Learning can take many forms, though. When I was young, I read science fiction books a lot. Isaac Asimov, Ray Bradbury, Robert Heinlein. One of the greatest sci-fi writers, Arthur C. Clarke, posited Three Laws. The third law was, "Any sufficiently advanced technology is indistinguishable from magic." He was thinking specifically of technology, of course. Meaning, that if we touched down in the Middle Ages with the technology we have today, we would appear as magicians to everyone."

"Sure, of course."

"But, I believe the same is true of spiritual advancement. When someone who has chosen to be more advanced in this lifetime comes along, the rest of us look at him, and declare his deeds to be miracles. But, healing people, stopping people from killing people, like I did yesterday, those things are no more magic than a tank would have been a thousand years ago. Make sense?"

Laura smiled. "I suppose. I have this feeling that like everyone else, I am going to be dissecting this interview for years to come. I don't suppose you could just give me some of this miraculous perspective you have, and make it easier on me, could you?"

Laura laughed a bit at the idea, but Nathaniel said, "I could, yes."

Laura's eyes flew wide. "Honestly?"

"Honestly."

"Would you?"

"I will, but I have to warn you. It will be a temporary glimpse, and for a time after, this reality will seem drab."

Laura nodded. "Thank you for warning me, but I'd like to see it."

Nathaniel reached his hand out. Laura debated for several seconds, but then, in one swift motion, offered her own. Nathaniel held her hand and closed his eyes. He released her.

Laura sat up, jolted by an electricity that ran through her body and straightened her spine. "Oh!" If her eyes had been wide before, they were now flung open as far as they could go. They were alight with the vastness of the universe. She didn't blink, she didn't focus. A moment later, she said it again, softly. "Oh." A single tear spilled onto her cheek. Ever so slowly, the light in her eyes faded, until she looked herself again.

The silence stretched out, seconds into minutes, as the camera continued to roll, the one-eyed machine of record. Laura didn't move, didn't speak.

Fully three minutes of silence later, she regained the power of speech. "I ... I don't know what to say. When will I feel that, *know* that again?" She stared at Nathaniel, her eyes burning with a need she never knew she had.

"That's what awaits us all, in good time."

"Whoo. I feel so strange." She used the sheaf of papers to fan herself, as though the studio lights had just now become hot.

"Your consciousness was far away. Think of your daughter. Hold her in your mind. That will help bring you back here."

"Yes. Yes. Good." She absent-mindedly wiped the tear away.

"Any more questions I might have had are gone, lost in the ether. I'll just ask, what's next for you? Where do you go from here?"

"Home. I'm going home."

Chapter Thirty-Eight

In their borrowed car, Nathaniel behind the wheel, heading north on I-5, Violet said, "Well, that was certainly interesting."

"My big star turn, direct from the media hotspot of Eugene, Oregon, and that's all you can say? Interesting?" Nathaniel smiled at his mother. "Thank goodness that is the only time I'm ever going to do that. Put a camera in front of me, and I turn into a blabbermouth. Laura seemed to think that people will dissect what we talked about for years to come, but I think everyone will soon be flipping over to those *Criminal Minds* reruns she mentioned."

"I'm sure some people will, yes. Not everyone is ready for what you've told them, are they?"

"No, we all travel our own path up the mountain, at our own chosen speed. That's the way the universe is designed. Who am I to question it?"

"Do you think it was wise to announce we were going home? That program will likely air before we can get there."

Nathaniel put his hand on his mother's arm, "They've had my house staked out since the bombing. They weren't going anywhere. There just might be a few more of them, now." He took his eyes off the road for a moment to glance at his mother. "I won't hide anything anymore. That's what I realized as I was talking to Laura. That's what I had to learn in this life—to simply *be* and be willing to accept the consequences, whatever they are. So, no more running, no hiding. Whatever's next, we'll face it head on."

They passed a sign that said, "Sally's Diner, featuring our World Famous Chicken Fried Steak, next exit."

Nathaniel looked at his mother and raised his eyebrows questioningly.

"Oh, fine. We might as well, the whole world knows where we're going anyway. Surprised we don't have a parade escort already."

They pulled off the freeway, found Sally's Diner and pulled into the parking lot. Nathaniel took a deep breath, threw the car door open, and said, "C'mon, I'm buying." He stepped out of the car, patted his pockets, and said, "Ooops. Forgot that I gave all my money to Laura. I guess you're buying after all."

"This goes a long way toward explaining why I don't date any more. Men always forgetting their wallets."

"The least I can do is hold the door open for you then," Nathaniel said, whooshing the door open with a "ding." No one noticed them as they stood by the "Please Wait To Be Seated" sign.

A moment later, a heavy-set woman with painted on eyebrows and a big smile said, "Just the two of you tonight? Please tell me you're not two chaperones of a bus full of hungry basketball players. I don't know if I can survive another one."

"No, just the two of us," Nathaniel said.

"Follow me, got the best seat in the house lined up for you." She turned halfway, then stopped so abruptly that Violet nearly stepped on her. She didn't say anything, though, just gave her head a little shake and led them to their table.

Following, Violet leaned over to Nathaniel and whispered, "And so it begins."

Once they were seated, she said, "The special tonight is meatloaf with all the fixin's, and of course, there's—"

"—the World Famous Chicken Fried Steak?" Nathaniel guessed. The way he said it, you could almost hear the capital letters.

"Ah, you've seen our billboard. Yes, the chicken fried steak is excellent."

"Any vegetarian recommendations?"

"Find a different restaurant?" the waitress said, but laughed. "Yeah, sure hon, this is Oregon, land of the tree huggers. There's a whole section of the menu for you guys."

After she was gone, Nathaniel leaned over to Violet and said, "I believe I have just been identified as part of a group. Vegetarians. 'You guys.' I feel like I've joined a club."

"You go ahead and be a vegetarian, honey. I'm having the chicken fried steak."

Five minutes later, they had placed their orders and were drinking coffee out of heavy ceramic cups.

Nathaniel smacked his lips. "So much better than what they serve at the Middle Falls police station."

A young woman with a toddler on her hip tentatively approached their table.

"Here we go," Violet said softly.

"Mr. Moon?" the young woman said. She had a sensible, short haircut, and the bags under her eyes told the story of several sleepless nights. Nathaniel glanced over her shoulder and saw an even younger child in a car seat behind her.

"Yes, but call me Nathaniel."

She blushed a little and said, "I'm so sorry to bother you. My husband Billy told me not to, but I saw your meals hadn't arrived yet."

"It's no bother at all."

"I don't need anything. I just want to tell you that what you did means so much to us. There's so much bad news, it makes us scared for our kids sometimes. I told Billy the other night that if we saw one more school shooting, we were going to homeschool our kids. I'm getting so I'm afraid to let them out of our sight." She glanced down at the toddler, which Nathaniel now saw was a little girl. "Seeing what you did, just meant so much to us. It gave us hope that there's good things in the world, too."

"What's your little girl's name?"

"Oh, this is Bethany. That's my husband Billy. And Billy Jr. is in the car seat over there," she said nodding over her shoulder.

"How does Bethany do with strangers?"

"Oh, she loves everybody. Why? Do you want to hold her?"

In answer, Nathaniel held his arms out for her. Bethany leaned away from her mother's hip and into Nathaniel's hands. He brought her to him, and said, "Hello, sweet Bethany. Very pleased to meet you." In answer, Bethany laid her cheek against Nathaniel's chest, then reached up and wrapped her messy wet hands around Nathaniel's long hair and pulled.

"Oh, my gosh, I'm so sorry. She does that all the time. That's why I have this," she said, pointing to her own closely shorn locks.

Nathaniel laughed a little, freed his hair from Bethany's chubby fingers, and lifted her out to her mother. "Thanks for letting me hold her. I love these little ones."

"Of course you do," the woman said. "We already knew that. Oh, here's your food!" She stepped back away from their waitress, who was burdened with their dinners. "We won't bother you anymore. But, thank you. Sincerely."

As she turned, Nathaniel saw her stick her tongue out slightly at Billy Sr.

"She wasn't bothering you, was she?" their waitress asked.

"Oh, no. She was very sweet. She just let me hold her baby."

"Okay, just let me know if you have any trouble. We believe in letting people eat in peace, no matter how famous they are."

"Do you get a lot of famous people in here?"

"We had the Hager Twins in about ten years ago. You know, from *Hee Haw*?"

"Of course! I loved that show. I remember them well."

She sat their plates down on the table and looked thoughtful for a moment. "The man who was in those *Don't squeeze the Charmin* commercials was in, too. We get all kind of celebrities dropping in."

"Well, we appreciate the privacy, but please don't worry about us."

"You're sweet." She glanced over her shoulder at a man who had his phone out and pointed toward their table. "Jim, damn it, don't make me drop that phone in a sink of dirty dishes, now."

Jim guiltily put the phone down.

"Enjoy your meal, and let me know if you need anything else."

Half an hour later, they were safely out of the diner, and on their way north toward Middle Falls. Violet turned the rearview mirror so she could see if anyone had followed them, but there was nothing but miles of darkened road behind.

Before Nathaniel had a chance to say anything, Violet held up a hand, and said, "We're just lucky that no one in there was dying of something. If that place had been next to a hospital, we'd still be there while you were setting broken bones and curing cancer."

"You worry too much about stuff, Mom. Let it go. We've made the decision. That was the hard part. Now, we just get to live."

Chapter Thirty-Nine

As they drove, they called Jon and Melissa and left them a message, asking if they would meet them at the house.

Jon called the burner phone back a few minutes later. Violet answered it and put the call on speaker. Jon said, "Take it slow coming down toward your house. It's quite a parade, but they'll part like the Red Sea before Moses' staff, if you give them a chance."

"Anybody give you any trouble?" Violet asked.

"Nah. Unless you count having several thousand questions shouted at you simultaneously as trouble. I'm a big boy. Didn't hurt me at all."

"See you soon, brother. Why don't you guys open a bottle of wine, and feel free to put Katie to bed in my room. I don't think I'm going to sleep tonight."

Nathaniel and Violet rolled down the road that led to his house a little before midnight. As promised, there was a long parade of cars and television trucks parked along the shoulder leading to his house. As they approached, several of the trucks lit up the area with klieg lights.

Nathaniel squinted against them and said, "I wonder if they do that to every car coming down the road, or if they know it's me? If they do it to everyone, I'm going to have to bake something and take it around to the neighbors by way of apology."

Nathaniel slowed the car to a crawl and inched past all the vehicles. They had left his driveway unblocked, so he was able to drive right up to his house. As soon as he stepped out, the barrage of questions that

Jon had warned him about were shouted at him. Nathaniel noticed that everyone had stayed off his property, though.

Nathaniel looked at the large graveled area he had to the left of the driveway. "Mom, go on inside. I'll be there in just a minute."

Before Violet could protest, Nathaniel walked into the glare of the lights, holding his hand up to shield his eyes. He ignored the questions which were machine gunned at him, but held up his hand, asking for quiet. The onslaught continued for a time, but as he looked patiently, and quietly, at them, they eventually slowed to a trickle.

"Thank you. I'm not going to answer any questions. I gave an interview earlier today, and I'm going to let that stand as my statement." That brought a renewed energy to the crowd of reporters, who began shouting at him again. Nathaniel smiled patiently at them, and raised his hand again, waiting for them to wind down.

"However, you guys are kind of making a nuisance of yourselves by blocking the road out here, and blinding every poor approaching driver with your lights. So, you can all come and park on my property over here." He pointed toward the half acre of gravel he was intending to turn into a massive sports court once he had saved up the money. "Please keep it to the gravel area. Sorry I don't have a port-a-potty. You'll have to figure that out for yourselves. There's a Texaco station with clean rest rooms about two miles down the road. Have a good night."

With a wave, Nathaniel turned and made his way back to his house. Behind him, vehicles were starting up and jockeying for the best spots on the gravel.

When Nathaniel stepped through his front door, Jon and Brutus were waiting for him in the entry way. Brutus stretched up and put his paws on Nathaniel's shoulders and sniffed him deeply. He sneezed, decorating his shirt with dog snot. "I know. I feel the same way," Nathaniel answered, hugging Brutus close. "Sorry I had to leave you, boy."

"Tell me you didn't invite those people onto your property. That's crazy," Jon said.

"Just trying to make it easier on the neighbors. They've always been good to me—letting me hike across their land, bringing fresh milk over. No way I could repay their kindness by jamming up the only road to their house." Nathaniel grinned. "It's not like they were going to go away."

"True enough. I just hate to see you so exposed." Jon wrapped him in a bear hug, squeezing him tight. "I know I told you, but thank you. For everyone, but especially for our Katie."

"It's all good. I don't feel exposed at all. This has been bothering me all my life, this idea of needing to hide. Now it doesn't. The dreading is so much worse than the actual event. It's so often that way, isn't it?"

"I suppose, and I'm glad you feel that way," Jon said, systematically pulling the shades down on the windows around the house. "Because I'm selfish, and even if I knew it was going to ruin your life, I would have asked you anyway. I'm not much of a friend."

"Take comfort. I did think it was going to ruin my life, and I chose to do it anyway. Now, it's been my salvation, in an odd way." Nathaniel peeked through the blinds at the trucks idling out past his driveway. "I'll deal with them in the morning. I'd rather be in here, nice and cozy in the perfect little house you built for me, than sitting in an idling truck all night. Hey, did you open that bottle of wine?"

"Not yet."

"I'll grab a bottle. I've been saving something for a special occasion, and I think this is it." He opened the recessed pantry, which stayed cool year-round, and rummaged around before he emerged with a bottle. "This is supposed to be a tremendous Chardonnay, and they grow the grapes in the valley just up the road. Mom? Interested in a bit o' the grape?"

"After the day we've had? God, yes."

"I thought so. Grab us some glasses, will you?"

Melissa came close to Nathaniel and put her arms around him. She laid her head against his chest and broke down for a few moments. Nathaniel rocked her gently back and forth. "Nothing to worry about now. She's safe and sound and sleeping right in there."

Melissa looked at him through teary eyes and kissed him on the cheek, then sat down at his long dining room table—the biggest piece of furniture in his small house.

Violet appeared with four wineglasses. Nathaniel corkscrewed the bottle open and poured until it was empty. He lifted his own glass and said, "Good health, love, and laughter." The four tapped glasses and drank deeply.

"I can see this is going to be a several-bottle kind of night," Nathaniel said, returning to the pantry for another bottle and setting it on to the table next to its dead comrade.

The four of them sat up for hours, talking, reminiscing, and re-membering the life they had shared. Violet remembered the first day Nathaniel had brought Jon home, how he was so big she thought he must have been a friend of Andi's. That stirred a whole stretch of mem-ories about Andi—her eternal smile, her proclivity for getting into trouble, and most of all, the love she had for Violet and Nathaniel.

Jon poured the rest of another bottle of wine into everyone's glass-es, and held up his own. "To Andi, she will never be forgotten." The clinked their glasses again, and Melissa said, "I feel so sad that I never got to meet her. I always thought Jon might have had a little crush on her." She turned her head questioningly at Jon, who blushed a bit, but didn't answer.

A little after 2:00 a.m., Violet was the first casualty to sleep. She drifted off to lay down in the guest room. An hour later, Melissa gave up the fight and joined Katie in Nathaniel's room, and it was just Jon and Nathaniel. Just before dawn, Jon said he was going to sit on the couch and rest his eyes for a minute. Thirty seconds later, he was snoozing.

Nathaniel sat quietly for a few minutes, then picked up the empty wine bottles and put them in the glass recycling. He washed the wine glasses while he put on a pot of coffee to brew. When it was done, he poured himself a cup and stepped out on his porch to watch the sun rise. As soon as he did, there was stirring in the trucks, and a dozen cameras were aimed at him. Overnight, the crowd had swelled.

It wasn't just news trucks and reporters any more. Definite factions had sprung up in different areas. The news teams had their spot on the gravel. On one side of the fence that ran along his driveway, people were waving at him and holding signs that read things like, "My little girl needs you!" or "I believe in you, Nathaniel." On the other side, the crowd was grimmer. Their signs read things like, "Anti-Christ" and "Religion doesn't like you either, Satan."

Nathaniel took it all in, watched the sun rise up over the distant hills, and lifted his cup of coffee in a salute to all of them.

Chapter Forty

After enjoying his cup of coffee, Nathaniel checked in on everyone, and saw they were all still sleeping.

"Good enough," he said to himself.

He lifted the coffee pot, grabbed a stack of Styrofoam coffee cups from the pantry, and went back outside. He strolled over to the news reporters. "Morning, boys and girls, it's another beautiful day in the neighborhood. Any of you intrepid reporters and hardworking techs want some coffee?"

"Oh, hell yes," the man closest to him said.

Nathaniel reached the stack of cups out to him, then poured a steaming hot cup for him. "There you are, sir. This is an odd situation, but we don't have to live like savages, right?"

The next woman, a reporter dressed in a gray jacket and skirt, said, "I don't suppose you have any cream and sugar for it?"

Nathaniel nodded. "For you, it's already in there."

She tasted it suspiciously, but then smiled broadly. "You are my kind of man."

Nathaniel moved down the line, offering a cup and filling it for each person that wanted one. After half a dozen people asked for a cup, the whispers began down the line. "The pot never empties." One wag said, "Those cups are like the *500 Hats of Bartholomew Cubbins*. No matter how many he takes off, the stack stays the same."

And so it was.

Nathaniel continued down the line, offering coffee to everyone. One man, a tall, lanky cameraman wearing a loud Hawaiian shirt, tasted the coffee and said, "That's a damn fine cup of coffee."

Nathaniel nodded in acknowledgement and said, "Sorry, I didn't think to make cherry pie to go with it."

When he reached the end of the line, he looked back over the twenty or so people who were all drinking coffee and chatting, like they were lined up waiting for a barbecue to start. Several of them even forgot to train their cameras on Nathaniel for the moment.

Next, he walked over to the line that he had already begun to think of as *The Believers*. Unlike the news group, they didn't have a shred of ironic detachment. Their eyes were wide, their lips were smiling, and they all knew they were not only in the presence of greatness, but holiness.

None of them had the temerity to ask for their coffee in any way other than black, but nonetheless, every cup Nathaniel poured them was exactly to their taste. This did nothing to lessen their belief.

Eventually, he came up on a woman who declined the coffee, but held her child out to him. She said only one word. "Please."

Nathaniel handed the cups and coffee pot to the next person in line and reached out his arms and held the young girl, who was no more than four or five, in his arms. Blonde curls framed her pale face. Her eyes had been closed, but when Nathaniel held her, she opened them a bit. Pale green eyes flecked with gold. She smiled timidly at him. Nathaniel rocked her slightly, pushed her hair away from her face, and murmured something so quietly to her that no one could hear.

The girl's eyes flew open wide and focused on his face. She nodded. Nathaniel hugged her to him for a brief moment, then handed her back to her mother. "She'll be fine, now. She's a very sweet girl." As he gave the girl back, his hand brushed against the mother. "Oh. You too?"

Tears streamed down the woman's face. She nodded. "I'm so afraid. Not of dying, but of leaving her alone. I wish I could be here for her."

Nathaniel brushed her tears away, letting his hand rest on her cheek. "And now, you will."

He retrieved the pot and continued his rounds. In this group, a different sick person popped up every few feet, imploring him to heal them. He had a brief conversation with each of them, then laid hands on them, and they were well. Eventually, that which is miraculous might become commonplace, but on this morning, it did not.

Seeing the healings and the miracle of the coffee pot, a few people from the third section moved over to the *Believers* area. The longer he lingered with the group, more and more people parked up the road and walked up, joining in. The crowd swelled.

Two hours later, he had done what he could for everyone in the second group and turned toward the waves of hatred and vitriol that washed over him from the other side of his driveway.

He held out the coffee pot, still half-full, hopefully.

"Tools of the Devil!" a small woman shouted at him. "Get thee behind me, Satan!" Small drops of spit flew from her lips as she yelled, showering the back of the man in front of her.

Nathaniel set the pot and cups down in the grass and opened his arms wide. "Do any of you need anything? Is there anything I can do for you?"

An old man, bent and wizened, leaning on a cane and in obvious pain, stepped out from behind a beefy man in overalls. The old man locked eyes with Nathaniel. "I have something for you, Nathaniel."

"Hello, Mr. Creech. Thank you for coming. I've been waiting for you."

Chapter Forty-One

F ar behind him, Nathaniel heard the door to his house open. He glanced over his shoulder and saw Violet step onto the porch. Nathaniel waved to her that everything was fine, but over her shoulder, she called to Jon, who also appeared on the porch, rubbing the sleep out of his eyes. Violet and Jon fell into a deep conversation, casting worried glances at Nathaniel.

He turned his attention back to Cyrus Creech, who had been speaking, though Nathaniel hadn't been paying attention.

"—and I believed you were one of God's true miracles! But I know different now. No true creature of God would waste these gifts as you have done. Now I know who you are. You are evil incarnate. You ruined my life."

Creech was dressed in his best black suit, left over from when he was a powerful man in his community. The jacket hung on him as though it was on a coat hanger. The lines of the shoulders went halfway to his biceps. The sleeves were past his knuckles, and the pants only stayed up because the belt cinched it tight.

"Your life isn't ruined, Mr. Creech. You are exactly where you should be, just as I am, and just as we agreed long ago, in the time that was hidden from both of us. It will be all right in the end. If it's not all right, it's not the end."

Creech's teeth pulled back, a grimace that reflected both physical pain and an immense pool of anger. "You are clever and manipulative, but I will not listen to you, I know who you are."

"We both know each other well, though we have barely spoken in this lifetime. Still, we are of the same family."

"Gah!" Creech screamed in frustration. He reached into the front pocket of his suit jacket and extracted the Walther 99. Around him, the crowd spread out. Their eyes grew wide, and they threw themselves away from him, leaving him as an island unto himself. The man in the overalls said, "Holy shit and shinola!" as he jumped back. Creech pointed the gun at Nathaniel's chest.

Behind him, Nathaniel noticed that Violet had recognized Cyrus Creech and had broken into a run, calling over her shoulder to Jon.

They'll never get here in time. Just as I want it. Sorry you have to see this, I don't know any other way. But, Cyrus, if you talk too long, you'll waste your opportunity, and you'll never get another.

Behind him, Violet closed in. She shouted something, but her voice was lost in the hubbub of sound.

Creech pulled the trigger with all his strength and the pistol spit bullet after bullet. The first found its intended target—Nathaniel's chest, destroying his breastbone and working its way into his lung. The kick of the pistol was too much for Creech and the nose of the pistol danced, dealing potential death in a random pattern. The second bullet also struck Nathaniel, shattering his collarbone and knocking him backwards.

The third bullet sailed high, harmlessly heading toward the foothills, but the fourth and fifth hit Violet dead center. The impact knocked her off her feet in a spray of blood. She landed on her back, staring up at the blue sky.

Jon jumped in front of Nathaniel and Violet while still running toward Creech. His goal was to take any of the bullets intended for them, but they danced around him, leaving him unscathed. A moment later, Jon tackled Creech, driving his shoulder into the old man. The sound of multiple bones breaking could be heard in the quiet, echoing aftermath of the gunshots. Jon snatched the gun away from him and turned to look at Nathaniel.

Nathaniel, improbably still standing, sat down heavily next to Violet.

"Is this what you chose too, Mother? Surely not. Let me fix you." He reached his hand out to her, but she shook her head, grabbed his hand and held it to her cheek.

"You're not the only one who makes things happen, right, son?" She closed her eyes tight and squeezed out tears. "I don't have any of your gift of foresight, but if I had known, this is exactly what I would have chosen. I knew you were planning this as soon as you gave that interview. It's okay. I am ready to move on to whatever is next." She tried to take a deep breath, but it just resulted in a deep, gurgling sound. "Thank you for choosing me to be your mother. I am blessed by you."

"Here," he said, touching her forehead, "at least let me take your pain away."

The tight grimace on her face eased. "Thank you. Will I see you again soon?"

"That's a mystery to me, too. My foreknowledge ends here, and I am glad. I'm tired of knowing."

Victoria smiled, then lapsed into unconsciousness, and Nathaniel felt her slip away. After she died, he closed his eyes, found her in the darkness, and rejoiced with her there. She hugged him, told him how she loved him, and went on with a happy laugh, to whatever was next for her.

Nathaniel opened his eyes, looked down at himself and laughed. The bullets had cut through his flannel overshirt and he saw that the powder blue *COME AT ME, BRO* shirt underneath was now stained red with his blood.

Wouldn't you know it? I'm going to die in this shirt.

Jon was still holding Creech to ensure he was disabled, when he saw Nathaniel trying to rise and rushed to his side.

"Please, Nathaniel. Don't do this. Don't leave. I will miss you so."

"You will miss my music. I've known you loved it all these years."

"That would be the only thing I wouldn't miss about you, brother."

"Every problem brings with it a lesson, and every lesson carries a price. I am happy to pay this price. Can you help me up?"

Puzzled, Jon did as he asked and lifted Nathaniel off the ground. Nathaniel threw his arm around his shoulder and took a few steps forward until he sat next to Creech.

"Yes, this is good. Thank you, Jon. You've been my warrior, my friend and my brother. I love you. Now, Mr. Creech and I have a small bit of unfinished business."

Jon eased Nathaniel to the ground, so he was right next to Creech. Far away, sirens sounded.

"Come on healer, heal yourself. I should have known you were a fake. They'll never try me for this, you know. I'll be dead before they can get a court date."

"No, you won't," Nathaniel said. He reached out to Creech, who tried to move away, but could not. Nathaniel grasped Creech's trembling hand. "Thank you, Cyrus. You have been my friend for many lifetimes, and I love you, too, for doing this. Soon enough, you will see that this is best for both of us." Nathaniel closed his eyes, smiled, then collapsed back into Jon's arms.

"No. Noooo!" Creech howled with a strength he hadn't possessed in many years. He rolled over and stood up nimbly.

Jon, still cradling Nathaniel, shouted, "Will someone grab him?"

Many did.

The sirens grew louder, just down the road, now.

"Take me back to Mom, will you, Jon? That's the right place for me."

Jon scooped Nathaniel up and carried him like a child, then laid him tenderly by Victoria's body.

"Thank you, brother. You'll know what to do from here."

Nathaniel heard the thundering of heavy paws as Brutus jumped down from the porch and ran at him with the same reckless abandon he always had. He skidded to an ungraceful halt.

Nathaniel smiled at him and put both arms around his neck. "You need a bath, boy." He pushed the hair away from Brutus's face and looked into his brown eyes. He laid his forehead against him and held him tight.

"I will miss you."

Finally, he let go, and laid back on the grass. Brutus whimpered, but only a bit, then laid his massive head across Nathaniel's wounds.

Nathaniel Moon closed his eyes and died.

Epilogue

Typically, sentencing hearings for criminals in their mid-seventies are a bit perfunctory. When you're that age, it can reasonably be assumed that anything more than a twenty-year sentence is the equivalent of a life sentence.

Jon West, who had been named executor in Nathaniel's will, pushed for the longest sentences possible. He appeared on talk shows, gave interviews, and publically asked the DA's office not to make any kind of a plea deal with Cyrus Creech. However, he did ask that they not seek the death penalty.

The outcome of the trial was never in doubt. Two dozen cameras had recorded the multiple murders, and there were hundreds of witnesses willing to testify to what they saw, including many of the reporters and TV people who were there. Cyrus Creech pled "Not guilty by reason of insanity," but the jury rejected that. They found him to be of sound mind and body.

In the end, the court sentenced Creech to life in prison with no chance of parole. In the case of a man who had been given a new lease on life, that meant a very long time stretched ahead of him, all of it to be spent behind bars.

As it turned out, Nathaniel had not only taken away only Cyrus's illness and granted him long life. Just as he had done for so many he had touched, Nathaniel had also taken the bitterness and anger away from him. Cyrus Creech became a model prisoner, and dedicated his life to assisting others who were incarcerated. He wrote a dozen books over that time, decrying the sickness of dogma and blindly following without questioning. They did not sell well. Most of the world preferred not to hear his message.

Jon and Melissa West, and eventually Katie, were Nathaniel Moon's strongest advocates. They guarded his name, words, and images carefully, giving it freely to causes they thought were worthy, and fighting those they did not. That, along with caring for a dog who never seemed to age, became their life's work.

As the recipients of all of Nathaniel's worldly goods, they established a trust in his name and turned his small house on the edge of the foothills into an artist's retreat where writers, sculptors, painters, and poets spent three months at a time creating their art. The stays were granted with no strings attached, with one exception: Nathaniel's music played in the house all day. A few of the more radical artists even came to like it.

Two years after Nathaniel perished, Jon also published a book: *My Life with Nathaniel Moon, the Reluctant Messiah.* The book told the story of their friendship, but long sections were dedicated to the life lessons Nathaniel had shared with him over the decades. It became a bestseller and was widely accepted as the gospel of Nathaniel Moon.

Inevitably, different factions sprang up that worshipped at the feet of the Middle Falls Messiah, but none of those ever got any oxygen from Jon or Melissa, as they knew the idea was anathema to Nathaniel.

As the years and news cycles passed, new stories came with them—the kidnapping of a judge, a Hollywood scandal, an airplane disappearing off the face of the Earth. With each new story, Nathaniel slipped further and further into the past, until eventually, he was consigned to history.

Nothing would have made him happier.

Epilogue Two

The moment Nathaniel Moon died, he opened his eyes in surprise. He was not in the dark stream where he had frolicked from life to life so many times before. Instead, he was in a dazzlingly white room, filled with white benches. A lovely woman with long, sandy hair and bangs sat beside him as though she had been expecting him.

She nodded at him, half-acknowledgement and half-bow. "Hello, Nathaniel."

"Carrie?"

"Of course. I wouldn't let anyone else come and welcome you."

He reached for her and hugged her close. He inhaled deeply, she smelled of sandalwood and fresh air. She was dressed in a long robe the color of pale moonlight on freshly fallen snow.

Nathaniel glanced down at himself and noticed he was wearing the same.

"You look wonderful, and it is so good to see you again. I remembered so much last life, but I had forgotten you. You've been so many things to me, over so many lifetimes," Nathaniel said.

"I know it felt like you remembered much, but you were clever when you decided to bring some memories into this final life with you. You still forgot enough that you could learn the lessons this life held for you."

Nathaniel took a moment to reflect back on his most recent life and saw the truth in Carrie's words. "You said, 'final life.' Does that mean I'm not going back?"

"Only if you want."

Again, Nathaniel paused to think. He shook his head. "No, I think I won't. There is so much beauty there, both in the place and the people, but I don't think so."

"I made the same choice. I understand."

"What do you do here, then?"

"I oversee those who watch the souls on earth, the Watchers, who feed the Machine." She blushed a little, looking almost shy. "I brought about a change here, so now I feel like I have to stay and see it through."

Nathaniel laughed a little, nodding in appreciation. "You always were a rabble rouser, in your own quiet way. So, what's next for me?"

Carrie held out her hand. A tiny ball of pure, iridescent light sat on her palm. She held it out to him. "A gift. This will take you wherever you want. The universe stretches out before you."

The next book in the Middle Falls Time Travel series, titled _The Emancipation of Veronica McAllister_,[1] will be available in May, 2018. You met Veronica at the end of her first life, when she encountered Nathaniel Moon.

Veronica felt like she had wasted her whole life, and was more than ready to give up. After hearing the last words from Nathaniel – "Know that you are safe. You are loved. You are perfect. No harm will ever come to you." – she died. In the opening chapter of her own book, Veronica will open her eyes back in her teenage life, all memories intact.

I hope you'll read her story to see whether she can find her strength, and overcome the many obstacles before her.

If you would like to preorder the book so that it shows up on your Kindle the moment it is published, you can order it here.[2] It's only $2.99 during its preorder period.

---

1.   http://amzn.to/2HkHegL
2.   http://amzn.to/2HkHegL

THE
EMANCIPATION
OF
VERONICA
McALLISTER

A Middle Falls Time Travel Story

SHAWN INMON

3

Author's Note

Thank you for joining me on this fourth trip through the world of Middle Falls, Oregon. This book is a little different from the first three in the series. I think of those first three books as a complete trilogy, and Nathaniel's story is a bit of a palate cleanser before I dive back into the more intertwined lives of the other characters in *The Emancipation of Veronica McAllister*[1].

By the way, if you would like to be on my *New Release Alert List*, you can join that here[2]. If you join, I will send you a copy of my book *Rock 'n Roll Heaven*[3] for free. If you want, you can even join, get your free book, and then leave. No hard feelings.

Nathaniel's story has been brewing inside me longer than anything else I've written. At age sixteen, I already knew I wanted to be a writer. It was then that I read *Dune*, by Frank Herbert. That book had a character named Alia Atreides, often referred to as *Alia of the Knife*. Through the mechanics of the plot, Alia gained consciousness in her mother's womb. That idea resonated with me and clung to my brain, never to leave.

Over the years, a number of other books and characters did the same – Donald Shimoda from Richard Bach's *Illusions,* Valentine Michael Smith from the great Robert A. Heinlein's *Stranger in a Strange Land,* and many more. They all went into the bouillabaisse that

---

1. *http://amzn.to/2HkHegL*

2.   http://bit.ly/1cU1iS0

3.   *http://amzn.to/1hYOtYX*

is my brain, and sat marinating. It must be about dinner time, as I am using a lot of food metaphors, I notice.

The year I turned twenty, I decided it was time for me to write my first novel. The only problem was, I wasn't anywhere near ready to write it, mostly because I simply hadn't lived enough to have anything to say, yet. That didn't stop me from trying, though, and so I struggled through a few chapters of a truly horrible novel called *The Man Who Is.* I am so happy no one else will ever see those pages.

Time moved on, as it inevitably does. Life, in the form of a career and a family, pushed any thought of writing out of my brain. I could never forget that "Man who Is," though. At the time, I thought his name was Jon, which you will recognize as the name of Nathaniel's best friend in this book.

Over the years, when I would see various situations come up, I would wonder, "How would that character respond to this." Essentially, I was practicing writing his story, even when I wasn't.

In the late 1980s, I began to notice how the world would hold its collective breath over a single news story—a baby down a well, a pro athlete charged with murder, a Long Island Lolita, a missing plane. As I watched the endless interviews with the people in the middle of these events, I noticed something they all had in common. None of them really had anything to say. That's when the idea occurred to me: what if my "Man who Is" was dropped down into the middle of a scene like that, and actually did have something to say.

So, the scene in this book where Laura Hall interviews Nathaniel was actually the first scene I had in mind for the book. I'd like to say the rest of the book wrote itself, but no, nothing about this book was destined to be that easy.

I had my own fifteen minutes in the spotlight, back in the fall of 1980. It was in the midst of the Iranian Hostage situation. I was working as a producer for radio station KAYO in Seattle. The host of the show I produced was none other than Laura Hall. I chose to pay tribute to her by naming the interviewer after her, because I admired her, and thought she was an incredible interviewer.

My job as producer was to line up guests, and then to man the phones and make sure everything ran smoothly during the show. Laura and I had a show meeting every Monday morning, and she would rattle off a list of people she wanted me to book. It was an incredible gig. I was only twenty years old, and I had the chance to meet and talk to people like Charles Schulz, Og Mandino, Buckminster Fuller, Abby Hoffman, and Ann Rule. At the end of each meeting, Laura would say, "Oh, and why don't you get me an interview with one of the hostages."

And then, we would both laugh, since the American hostages were being held under such tight scrutiny by their captors, she knew that was impossible. Right? I was young, and I didn't know yet what was impossible. So, I went to work on the task. I burned up the phone lines for months, looking for any way to get a number that might ring where the hostages were being held. Eventually, I came into contact with a British reporter, who gave me a phone number he thought had once rung into where the hostages were being held. He was certain it had been disconnected, long since.

I called the number. It wasn't disconnected. When I called, a male voice would answer in Farsi, rattle something off at me—I speak zero Farsi—and hang up the phone. We played that game for weeks, getting me nowhere. Eventually, I had the brilliant idea to pose as an overseas operator. This time, when the man answered the phone, I said, "This is the overseas operator. I have a person to person call for Bruce Laingen," in my most official voice. Mr. Laingen was the chief diplomat at the embassy at the time they were taken hostage.

The man on the other end didn't say anything, but this time, he didn't hang up. Instead, I could hear him set the phone down with a "clunk." I sat on hold, trying to calculate how much of my station's budget I was burning through every sixty seconds. Several long minutes later, a tired-sounding man picked up the phone and said, "Hello?"

I couldn't believe it! "Hello! Is this Bruce Laingen?"

"Yes…"

"This is Shawn Inmon, with radio station KAYO, in Seattle. Can I put you on the air with us?"

At first he demurred, but I am nothing if not a good salesman. I promised him that we wouldn't ask him any question that would get him in trouble with his captors, and that it would mean the world to all of America if we could just hear his voice. After a moment's pause, he agreed.

I was faced with a horrible dilemma. Laura was on the air in a room around the corner from me, and she couldn't see or hear me. In order to put Mr. Laingen on the air, I had to first put him on hold, which was pretty risky with our old phone system. I said a little prayer, hit the "hold" button, and burst into the studio. Laura looked at me like I was crazy, but I grabbed a commercial, slammed it into the cart machine, hit "play," and told Laura, "I've got Bruce Laingen on line three. You've got about twenty seconds to prepare for the biggest interview of your life."

I ran into the newsroom to make sure we had a tape rolling to capture the interview for history, and stood there with the nighttime news guys and watched in amazement as Laura, with zero preparation, conducted an incredible, insightful interview with Mr. Laingen.

It was the only interview any of the hostages gave in their 444 days of captivity.

To say that chaos ensued is an understatement. In the following twenty-four hours, I gave interviews to ABC, NBC, CBS, the BBC, Reuters, the Associated Press, United Press International, and two guys in black suits with badges that wanted to know how I had done it. I was contacted by a radio station in Los Angeles, who offered to triple my salary if I would come produce their afternoon drive show. I didn't take them up on it, by the way. I was twenty years old and scared to death to move to Los Angeles, where I knew no one. Instead, I happily accepted the $200 a month raise that KAYO offered me to stay.

Of course, my little moment in the spotlight was nothing like what Nathaniel experienced, and I didn't do anything dramatic, like swallow a bomb blast, but it did give me a perspective on what it's like when everyone wants a little piece of you, even for a just a day or two.

Not long after the interview, the station was sold, and I was fired by the new owners, because I was making $200 a month more than the other producers. Welcome to radio. Laura, meanwhile, did indeed give up her talk show and move to a small town in Oregon, so my art imitated life in that way as well.

And now, almost forty years after I first conceived it, my story of "The Man who Is" is complete, and I can let go of it. Thank you for having been a part of it.

As always, I owe many thanks to many people for helping me bring this book to life.

As he did in *The Life and Death of Dominick Davidner,* Dan Hilton was my editor for this book. His professional approach, excellent grasp of my grammatical quirks, and keen eye for details not only made this book better, but saved me from looking a fool from time to time. What more can you ask from an editor?

Linda Boulanger from *TellTale Book Covers* once again created the cover for the book. Sometimes it takes us many iterations to get a cover right, but the first cover Linda presented me was the one you see here. I knew it was perfect. She gives my books the outer face they show to the world, and I love and appreciate her for it.

I had two proofreaders for this book, Deb Galvan and Mark Sturgill. Why two proofreaders? Possibly because I make twice as many mistakes as authors do! Plus, Deb and Mark each approach the book from different perspectives. Deb is my grammar and extra spaces maven, and Mark is my fact-checker extraordinaire. I don't know what I'd do without them, so I intend to never find out.

I hope it doesn't show in the final product, but this was a difficult book for me to write. My best writer friend, Terry Schott, served as my alpha reader and suffered through many different iterations of the first half of this book, as I struggled to locate the line of the story I wanted to tell. His insight and honesty helped me to do just that.

Likewise, I used a team of beta readers, who read early drafts and made suggestions as to how the book struck them, and what could be done to improve it. They were invaluable, and I want to thank Jeff Hunter, Carmen Anslow, Barb Larson, Laura Heilman, Marta Rubin, Kerri Lookabaugh, Fay Barger, Jerry Weible, Craig Simmons, Jan Tanner, Dale Lewis, and Janice Friedman-Snyder for their input. If you read for me and I forgot to mention you, the blame is mine. Nathaniel Moon is the only near-perfect person around here.

As always, I want to save my biggest thank you for you. You are the reason I sit at the keyboard, exploring the dustiest corners of my imagination.

Shawn Inmon
Seaview, Washington
March, 2018

Other Books by Shawn Inmon

The Unusual Second Life of Thomas Weaver[1] – Book one of the Middle Falls Time Travel Series. Thomas Weaver led a wasted life, but divine intervention gives him a chance to do it all over again. What would you do, if you could do it all again?

The Redemption of Michael Hollister[2] — Book two of the Middle Falls Time Travel Series. Michael Hollister was evil in Thomas Weaver's story. Is it possible for a murderer to find true redemption?

The Death and Life of Dominick Davidner[3] – Book Three of the Middle Falls Time Travel Series. When Dominick is murdered, he awakens back in his eight year old body with one thought: how to find Emily, the love of his life.

Feels Like the First Time[4] – Shawn's first book, his true story of falling in love with the girl next door in the 1970's, losing her for 30 years, and miraculously finding her again. It is filled with nostalgia for a bygone era of high school dances, first love, and making out in the backseat of a Chevy Vega.

Both Sides Now[5] – It's the same true story as Feels Like the First Time, but told from Dawn's perspective. It will surprise no one that first

---

1. https://www.amazon.com/Unusual-Second-Life-Thomas-Weaver-ebook/dp/B01J8FBONO

2.   http://amzn.to/2wyUfCH

3.   http://amzn.to/2yTgHnk

4.   https://www.amazon.com/Feels-Like-First-Time-Story-ebook/dp/B00961VIIM

5.   https://www.amazon.com/Both-Sides-Now-True-Story-ebook/dp/B00DV5GQ54

love and loss feels very different to a young girl than it did for a young boy.

Rock 'n Roll Heaven[6] – Small-time guitarist Jimmy "Guitar" Velvet dies and ends up in Rock 'n Roll Heaven, where he meets Elvis Presley, Buddy Holly, Jim Morrison, and many other icons. To his great surprise, he learns that heaven might need him more than he needs it.

Second Chance Love[7] – Steve and Elizabeth were best friends in high school and college, but were separated by a family tragedy before either could confess that they were in love with the other. A chance meeting on a Christmas tree lot twenty years later gives them a second chance.

Life is Short[8] – A collection of all of Shawn's short writings. Thirteen stories, ranging from short memoirs about summers in Alaska, to the satire of obsessed fans.

A Lap Around America[9] – Shawn and Dawn quit good jobs and set out to see America. They saved you a spot in the car, so come along and visit national parks, tourist traps, and more than 13,000 miles of the back roads of America, all without leaving your easy chair.

A Lap Around Alaska[10] – Have you ever wanted to drive the Alaska Highway across Canada, then make a lap around central Alaska? Here's your chance! Includes 100 photographs!

6.   https://www.amazon.com/Rock-Roll-Heaven-Shawn-Inmon-ebook/dp/B00J9T1GQA

7.   https://www.amazon.com/Second-Chance-Love-Shawn-Inmon-ebook/dp/B00T6MU7AQ

8.   https://www.amazon.com/Life-Short-Collected-Fiction-Shawn-ebook/dp/B01MRCXNS3

9.   https://www.amazon.com/Lap-Around-America-ebook/dp/B06XY9GSWC

10.   https://www.amazon.com/Lap-Around-Alaska-AlCan-Adventure-ebook/dp/
      B0744CVWT4/ref=sr_1_4?s=digital-text&ie=UTF8&qid=1506966654&sr=1-4&key-
      words=shawn+inmon+kindle+books

Printed in Great Britain
by Amazon